To my 1981 students

at the Department of English and Literary Studies,

University of Calabar.

DOUBLE YOKE

A novel by

Buchi Emecheta

Ogwugwu Afor Books
An imprint of

OMENALA PRESS
London & Nigeria

An Ogwugwu Afor Book, 2018

ISBN: (Paperback) 978-1-911428-04-6

ISBN: (Ebook) 978-1-911428-06-0

www.omenalapress.co.uk
info@omenalapress.co.uk

Follow us on Facebook, Twitter and Instagram
@omenalapress

First Published in 1982 by Ogwugwu Afor Books

First Published by Fontana Paperbacks 1984

CONDITIONS OF SALE

Cover design by Victor Ehikhamenor

Printed in India by Imprint Digital Ltd

Contents

1. *The New Woman*

The new lecturer was very eloquent in her talk of reform - in what she would like to see done and in what she would like to see undone in the university in particular and in Nigeria in general. This, to the students of this new university of Calabar, a university which, because of its newness, attracted many, many weird lecturers was nothing new. There was for instance that funny law person who came a few years back and insisted on Nigerian lawyers doing away with what he called 'ridiculous wigs'. Wigs which to the Nigerian law students were the mark of their achievement. So the students, especially the fourth years had seen and heard it all before. What was new about this one was that she was a woman!

Not that the well-informed female was a new phenomenon in a country like Nigeria, in the early nineteen eighties, but the unusual thing about this one was that she was outspoken, almost as outspoken as the village women whose daughters had been to the UK and became been-tos and were now so perfect in hypocrisy. These been-tos had learnt to pretend to be ignorant as this was the only way they could get husbands, the only way they could survive in their romanticized ideas of femaleness. They spent so much of their time being women, that they lost sight of what their education was all about. Ete Kamba remembered a member of staff in the university who was rather sly and knew how to get her way usually began by introducing her talk with 'since I am not the pushful type' - she incidentally was the highest paid black female lecturer on campus, yet she was not the pushful type. The male students used to joke and say, 'I wonder what would happen if she were the pushful type'. But this new Miss Bulewao, did not sound pushful, rather the self-confident type. So sure of herself, so sure of her subject. Well she had written over six books on her subject, so she had reasons to be sure. But to the boys she was a marvel, and as for Ete Kamba he wished she were a man!

The other day when she came in to give one of her early lectures, the evening was mercifully cool, so the windows of lecture room 104 were all opened.

'Well, this is cool enough for our been-to madam,' remarked Esang.

The students had laughed. They looked around them and found that not only was the room cool, but that they were thirty or so students, less than they used to have for other courses.

'Have you noticed, boys, that there is no single female in this class and that we are so few in number even though almost the whole campus knew of Miss Bulewao's appointment.'

'We who are here are geniuses, budding geniuses,' Isa boasted. 'Others are frightened to come near her, in case they don't make it as writers.'

'Hmmm, I don't know about that, all I know is that fools rush in where...' Ete Kamba began.

'Oh, for God's sake, Ete Kamba, you mean girls on this campus are angels? Oh my God...' Esang broke in, holding his hands up in mock supplication. 'Oh my God,' he wailed again.

The whole class collapsed in laughter and the talk

about campus girls disintegrated into personal bickerings in uncouth language, punctuated by derisive, uneasy laughter. Some of the boys looked at Ete Kamba, rather uneasily, knowing that his case was a classic example. He pretended not to see the pointing fingers and the knowing nods. His particular case was well known on campus.

When Miss Bulewao entered with her masculine brief-case and quiet tread, the students were too full of their woes to see her. She was a very insignificant looking female - not the type the boys had imagined a writer to be. She was so ordinary, more like any mum, any farmer's wife. She stood there, looking at them, waiting for them to be quiet.

Soon an uneasy silence fell, as her presence became noticed. Some boys were really so worked up in their arguments, that their sentences hung in mid-air, when they suddenly turned and saw her standing there.

She smiled broadly and said, 'good evening, boys.'

They returned her greeting and she went on with her subject on Creative Writing. Most of the students were not unaware of the fact that with a subject like this, the work depended on themselves, but many would like to hear it said from the mouth of somebody who had actually made it in that field not only in Nigeria, but abroad. In fact Miss Bulewao was better known abroad than in her own country.

She was expanding on 'Comparative Literature in Africa' when the ceiling fan started to hiccough. The boys looked at each other and Ete Kamba could see Effiong lifting his shoulders and giving a shrug of despair. They knew what was going on, they knew what would happen soon. But the new lecturer did not. She carried on talking her subject.

NEPA people were at it again. NEPA people controlled the life style of many people in Nigeria. They gave and took away electricity lights whenever they felt like it. They always gave some unheard of excuses like the cables being overloaded, or that they were doing some repairs. Of course it was pointless trying to inform the rest of the population before the cuts, since there were so many in a typical day. And in a country where the telephone system was more of a decorative instrument than a functional one, warning the students, for instance, was thought out of this world. Most of the rich in the country however did not have to feel this. They had built generators into their lighting systems. Many even had automatic ones. Once NEPA took the light away, the generators took over. That was all right for the rich. Some of the important buildings in the University where the titled people worked, had generators as well, but the lecture halls, where students like Ete Kamba and his colleagues had to take their instructions, were not among the privileged buildings.

Ete Kamba suspected that most of these leaders feared the young ones. They therefore would see to it that they suffered what they had suffered when they were at different universities - those of them that ever saw the inside of a university that was.

The hiccoughing progressed to coughing and this was followed by a whizzing sound and the dimming of the light. Then the light fizzed out completely, plunging the room into sudden darkness. They were all aware of what was coming, yet its suddenness was

4

embarrassing to all. They felt embarrassed for Nigeria and they felt embarrassed for this new lady, who seemed so immune to all the changes around her.

There was the usual, 'ah, NEPA,' from all the boys. They noticed that she was desperately trying to joke about it, yet her nervousness permeated through. The fact that she was not used to this kind of darkness was apparent, try as she would to hide it. 'Sorry, madam,' some of the boys managed to say.

Ete Kamba got up, packed his loose sheets and at the same time groped for the torch he had left by the side of the metal desk, and switched it on.

'Oh, that is very kind of you, thank you so much,' the madam said. 'And . . . em, would you start your creative work by writing me an imaginary story of how you would like your ideal Nigeria to be. You realize, I hope that in subjects of this kind most of the work depends on you. If you practice writing hard enough, you may make it. But speaking personally, I think that any student of this department should know how to write creatively.'

They all thanked her and began to file out. They were used to the pitch African darkness of Calabar. One minute it was bright, the next dark. They were used to the unevenness of their compound surrounds - potholes here, open gutters there, a dangerous puddle at the other end. She, however, was not, this plump woman, who with her books had almost transformed herself into a superhuman being. But with the mere unreliability of the Nigerian power system, her own vulnerability was expressed.

'I will lead the way, madam,' Ete Kamba volunteered. He lighted her way with his torch over uneven pavements, potholes and swampy grass. Outside the university, he waited with her until a taxi was hailed to take her back to her hotel at the Vetas Guest House in the main part of Calabar. This was because she was new, and had not yet been given her own accommodation.

She had thanked him again as she glided into the cab. Ete Kamba noticed that though she was not skinny, and though she was not the type of the New Woman they had been taught to regard as beautiful, she knew how to handle herself together.

He stood there enjoying the feel of importance, the feeling that for a few minutes he had had to protect the most talked about female writer in Nigeria, and maybe in the whole of Africa. As her cab sped into the dark night, he picked his way back to his room on campus in Malabor. He was half way through the open space that separated the lecture halls from the students' hostels when he realized that his torchlight was still on. He quickly switched it off mumbling, 'Oh dear, what a waste.' He had thought that the battery in the torchlight would see him through the semester. But now with this new lady, and with NEPA's determination to make student's life as miserable as possible he doubted it very much. Still it was worth it, to be near such a creative writer!

2. Looking Back

The air conditioner hummed with irritating consistency. It gave out a cool dusty air, in repayment for its annoying noises. Students, librarians and research workers shuffled about under the pretext of looking for this or that, but in actual fact, they were only trying to ward off boredom and sleep. Air conditioners are very good, but they tend to lull one to sleep. They make the air so artificially cool. But one must not grumble about them; next to quinine, they are a must for tropical living.

Ete Kamba had chosen the reference section of his university library to try and work out the best way to tackle the assignment the new lecturer had given them. 'What type of Nigeria would I like to see?' He went round this title many times mouthing the words in the air. Had he got it right? Was that exactly what the lecturer, Miss Bulewao, wanted them to write about? He scratched his sweaty head several times, throwing his long legs this way and that, then shuffling on his seat in a desperate attempt to find an adept title for what he wanted to write. He knew what the subject was, but felt the title he could remember was not good enough.

He was still very young, only twenty-four, a fourth year final student in the English Department. After doing his Youth Corps, he hadn't the faintest idea what he would like to do. One thing he knew for sure was that if he made a good grade, he would come back to this same university to try and do a second degree in African Literature. But beyond all that, he did not want to think. And suppose he did not get a good degree? Well he would do his Youth Corps and go into administration. Teaching would have been the best thing, but all the students knew that teachers, including lecturers didn't command the type of respect they used to have in time long gone. His parents had told him that much. They even told him that there was a time in their small village at Mankong, near Calabar, when the school headmaster was almost the village overlord. They told him that after the king, the village headmaster was next. They even said that sometimes, because of his learning, he would outwit the king and his family, because the village headmaster could speak the English language very fast and knew how to get things from the Europeans who came to trade down the river mouth.

But all this had changed now. Everybody was educated. Now everybody spoke English and the language was no longer the preserve of the king's family or the family of the headmaster. So Ete Kamba knew that if he went back to his village and said he wanted to be a local teacher, his parents would not allow him to do so. They would remind him of all the sacrifices they had made to have him educated, and of all the hopes they had entertained the day he gained an admission to their one and only University of Calabar. To his parents, the fact that one had been to a university was the passport to a successful life. Well so it should be, if one knew what one would like to do.

But after seeing this new lecturer, the idea of using his knowledge of English to write suddenly occurred to him as a possibility; yet, as he had told Isa in the lecture room, maybe one has to be a genius to be able to create things on paper. Had he been a fool, as he had jokingly said in class? Was he really serious when he said that? Sometimes in jest, he had noticed that he had a way of speaking the truth. While she was here, this lady, he would try and make the most of her presence, and include the profession of writing as one of the possible careers he could take up.

He allowed his mind to wander into how gratifying such an occupation could be. To really produce a book, maybe a best seller, that people could read and even study as works of Literature, as the college now studied Miss Bulewao's books! He imagined himself coming up to a platform and telling his listeners - students of Literature and reporters how he managed to write and why he had to write. He was shrugging his shoulders in his effort to tell his listeners that it was a simple thing when he knew that it was far from easy. That would be his attitude, to make it all look so simple. He was not going to deter any aspiring person from becoming a writer, if they wished to be, just as Miss Bulewao was doing. But then the reality crashed into his thoughts. He was wishing to be as successful as a woman: he was wishing to adopt the method used by an ordinary woman in the field of Arts! How low could one sink?

A clumsy student dropped a big 'Climate of Africa Atlas' on the floor. The bang it made woke everybody, and heads were raised. One girl in a red English silk dress with hair that had been so straightened that it shone, frowned. The noise had disturbed her, but the most disturbing was the dust the fallen Atlas had raised. The Atlas itself was very dusty, so much so that the blue cover could only be imagined from its grey overcoat of dust. The floor, cemented, was equally dusty, though the cleaners would tell any student who dared ask them why, that they had cleaned the place and that the dust they were seeing was the dust that had simply piled up during the day. So hard to believe sometimes, some of these stories, but one must not allow oneself to think too much about things like that. Ete Kamba always carried a large handkerchief anyway, to dust most of the library chairs before he sat down.

Now the dust was everywhere and before anyone could open their mouths to protest, everything suddenly went dead. The light was off, this time with unwarning suddenness. The silence that fell on all of them was tangible. When the whirring background of the air conditioner stopped like that, it felt as if life itself stopped. So those who would have protested about the noise did not know whether to start with NEPA, the cleaners or even the student. Apparently they all felt like Ete Kamba, and gave up, it would have been such a wasted emotion.

Ete Kamba kept his seat however. There were not enough working areas for students, to the extent that if one could manage to secure a place in the reference section with its wide tables, one was lucky. He would not write now, but while waiting for the light to come on, would think of the subject he was going to write about, so that when the light came, the ideas would have been carefully formed in his head.

One of the things the lady lecturer had said was that they should all start with the subject they knew best. She had also mentioned that oneself was always a very good topic to start writing about. Nigeria belonged to almost ninety million people, but he, Ete Kamba, belonged to himself and nobody else was going to be interested in what he had suffered and been through. The reason that he now wished this lecturer had been a man not a woman; the reason that he was now beginning to hate university life and why he sometimes entertained the idea of being a lecturer if he could make it, was simply to revenge what Professor Elder Ikot of the Cultural had done to him and his childhood sweetheart, Nko. Yes, that was enough reason for wanting to work hard, to take it out on future students. But that funny lady lecturer who preached Religion in Humanities had told them repeatedly that such thoughts were evil. He believed her to the extent that he had again attended one of their gospel singing and prayer meetings. He did not know what exactly he was looking for, but definitely not Professor Ikot on the platform. The professor was not only preaching but the Spirit of God took hold of him and again he started to speak in tongues, just the way he acted the first time Ete Kamba and his friends, Isa and Akpan saw him. That first night they all had been impressed with him and wondered how it had been possible for a professor to perform such wonders and still maintain the artificial, mystified air which most African professors had about them. Ete Kamba knew that they had to maintain that air. It was part of their survival armour. If they allowed themselves to become like other people, people would realize that they did not really know that much. But Professor Ikot of the Cultural was not frightened of looking common, because on that first evening, he claimed that it was God working through him.

The hall of prayer suddenly became stuffy when Ete Kamba heard Professor Ikot making the claim about the Holy Spirit again. Ete Kamba had walked out - to sit there and listen to Ikot, in his linen trousers which somehow emphasized his rapidly decaying appearance, speaking the word of God and knowing what the professor had done to him and his childhood sweetheart Nko, was too much. He could not take it. He stopped going to such places altogether. Now all he did was sometimes to visit the Neutral near-orthodox hymn singing and prayer thing they had every Sunday on campus. Once one had been brought up in a home where everybody went to church on Sundays, it was always difficult to shake off the habit. Ete Kamba did not mind. As long as there was water for bath at Malabor, putting on a white shirt and going to take part in hymn singing was not a bad way to spend Sunday mornings when the library was not opened. So, despite the preachings of Dr Mrs Edet from Humanities, Ete Kamba still harboured a grudge against Professor Ikot.

Or maybe if he could not be a professor himself because of the stiff formal exams most of which one would not need to remember once one had obtained one's certificates and safely tucked into a cushy job in a university corner, he could use the opportunity of this new lecturer to write about it. Get his revenge the civilized and academic way. He would write and tell the outside world that masses in the university campuses are oppressed. That on campuses like Malabor, four, five or even six students sometimes have to share a room, whilst young and sometimes unmarried senior lecturers have three bedroom houses and flats. That not being satisfied with that, they sometimes did steal their girlfriends. Just like Professor Ikot had done to his Nko. Yes he would write about that. He had nothing to lose but the chains which now bound his thoughts. Try as he would, Nko kept coming in to his thoughts.

And, as if in answer to his secret prayers, the hum of the air conditioner announced the on-coming lights. The lights flickered rather uncertainly at first, and then came into life. The air conditioner started its monotonous hum, all the students present bent to their papers once more, grateful that NEPA had taken only thirty minutes from their working time.

Ete Kamba put his biro on to a clean sheet of paper. He was going to tell the world how it all had been, between him and his Nko, until Professor Ikot came into their lives.

3. Boy Meets Girl

It was a special thanksgiving day. A local girl who had been studying hair-dressing in Aba had passed her examination, and had come to the church this Sunday morning to give thanks. The announcement had gone on for weeks, and Ete Kamba was simply curious to see what the service would look like. This girl, Arit, had been extra lucky because the special Minister had come all the way from the capital in Calabar to administer holy communion. So Arit was going to have a great audience for her hair-dressing thanksgiving service.

All Arit's distant relatives had come to the church. All the friends of the family had been there. The church was packed. And the God's minister, seeing such a great crowd, was inspired. He would read out the verse of each hymn, he would expand on it, and then hum it for the choir who would start the songs with their bearded gourds, their sambas, their gongs, and the congregation would clap. Some, who could not read, had the words shouted to them. So the music was very slow, but enjoyable. Who wanted a hurried service on a day like this anyway? To Ete Kamba's family, Sundays were for the church, so staying three to four hours in the House of the Lord was the least they could do to thank God for His Mercies.

When it came to the actual thanksgiving, each member of Arit's family insisted on going to the Lord separately, and some of them would want smaller change from the ten Kobo pieces they had given, and

15

the minister would not let anyone come without a special hymn to dance to the altar with. Ete Kamba caught himself yawning and stretching. Saliva spurted out of his mouth and he quickly looked around him to make sure that nobody was watching.

But she was watching, this thin little girl from the next pew. She covered her face with her hymn book, but the corners of her eyes had caught Ete Kamba and his yawn. She smiled and looked away quickly. She could not look at Ete Kamba again, partly because she was shy, but especially because Ete Kamba had never stopped looking at her, watching her. The service did not seem too long after that.

After the church service, the intensity of the sun forced most people to make for their homes very, very quickly. But Ete Kamba was determined to find out where this girl came from. He had been born in this village, so he knew everybody. But this girl was new. She did not come from this part. Ete Kamba was going to find out.

He heard his mother's tired voice calling him to come home so that they could have enough rest before the evening service, but he pretended not to hear. She gave up calling and walked home with his younger brothers and sisters.

Ete Kamba stayed behind pretending to help the choristers put away their robes and things. The lay reader smiled on seeing him. As Ete Kamba had been one of the choristers before he gained an admission to the Government Secondary School in the capital, he was the pride and joy of the whole community. He could do no wrong. So they were pleased that he was helping.

Most people were greeting and congratulating Arit on her success. Some were asking her whether she was going to open a salon or whether she was going to give her customers African hairdos. Ete Kamba heard Arit say very, very loudly that the lady who trained her in Aba was a been-to, and that she had been taught how to make African hair look European. She could straighten, she could blow, she could weave, she could curl and she could wash with shampoo. Many people opened their eyes. Arit had really made it. But who was going to patronize her, Ete Kamba thought? Not women like his mother, who still had their own farms to work on and who spent three quarters of their time sweating on their cocoyam patches. Arit would really have to relearn all she had learnt from her been-to madam in Aba to survive in Mankong.

Ete Kamba was temporarily distracted from the object of his quest. He seemed to have lost her for a while but on lifting his eyes he saw her standing waiting for something, expectant, with a near vacant look on her face under the orange tree. Ete Kamba who on other occasions was usually shy and self-conscious seemed drawn by a force whose power was beyond his. He went to her, and she smiled at him. She had apparently seen him coming and it almost looked as if she was waiting for him.

'Hot afternoon,' Ete Kamba blurted out, rather stupidly.

'Yes, it is very hot. Maybe we shall have rain soon.'

'That would be nice... em, the rain I mean.'

'Yes, the rain would be nice,' she echoed. And somehow the way she said it sounded so silly to both of them that she looked into his eyes and he looked into hers and they both started to laugh.

They were still laughing when a woman with a loud lappa and matching head-tie shouted, 'Nko, Nko, come on we have to go to their house, Nko!'

'Yes, Nma,' the girl answered, as she patted gently her headscarf to make sure it covered her forehead before stepping out of the shade of the orange tree into the hot sun.

'You are one of the party?' Ete Kamba managed to ask.

'Yes, my mother is Arit's mother's distant cousin. We are all here for the thanksgiving.'

'From Nbamkpa?' Nko nodded and went quickly to her mother.

Ete Kamba at eighteen was not unlike most boys of his age. When boys of that age are determined to get to the root of an object, only earthquakes or similar catastrophes can stop them. Ete Kamba never liked Arit. She was only a year or so older than he was. But her family had a way of attracting so much undeserved publicity to themselves. He never let her know, but he always avoided her. As children they had sung in the same church, sat on the same pew, but somehow Ete Kamba was never curious about this girl. He had been invited to the big party he knew would follow the church thanksgiving. In fact everybody in their village of Mankong was invited. But he was not really keen on going. He had told himself that he was going to fish and read and even dodge the evensong. But not now. He would like to see Nko again before she went back to her village. Not that Nbamkpa was a long way from the village of Mankong. The villagers of Mankong were until about four years before cut off from the rest of their Ibibio people. But four years ago, after the local engineer who had been given the contract to build a bridge joining the village to the mainland had been eventually sent to jail, and the contract given to a Jewish firm, the bridge was eventually built and Mankong was now joined to the mainland. It could have taken him only two hours on his father's bicycle, or thirty minutes by the motor boat that went every hour on the river. He knew all that. He also knew that Nbampka was smaller than Mankong, but he would look ridiculous if he walked in going from house to house asking for a girl named Nko. Nko was a common name for girls in Mankong and Nbampka. So he would have to go to Arit's noisy party.

During the midday meal, a sudden fear seized him. Suppose Nko and her mother had decided to leave before he was able to find out more about her? A fear of the type he had never experienced before overtook him, so much so that he shivered and gulped his food. Suddenly his hunger was abated. He got up. He had had enough.

His father's practiced eye did not miss a thing. Since Ete Kamba had gained admission into the elitist government school, he no longer ate with his mother and the younger members of his family. He now ate with his father. His mother would serve them, the men of the house on a special collapsible table they had bought from a carpenter in Calabar. She would then spread on it her one clean table cloth. Then she would bring their food, mainly garri and soup, in very clean but plain imported plates and a metal bowl of water to wash their hands with. She usually left the room after saying, 'Please enjoy your dinner,' Ete Kamba's father never answered. He would frown and look at the food from side to side in a boring way as if he was being forced to eat sick. But only a few minutes afterwards, the food would have almost disappeared, and the soup licked with his little shaved head held on one side of his shoulder.

He was still in the process of garri swallowing when Ete Kamba stood up so suddenly that he almost upset the precariously balanced table in his eagerness. His father rolled his tiny dark eyes slowly upwards to look at his son, a son who at eighteen was already a head taller than him. He arched his brows and had a lump of garri in the mid-air ready to be forced down his throat to meet many of its predecessors. Then he stated, 'Son, I am sure you have cockroaches in your shorts. Go and taken them off, and put on a lappa so that you can enjoy your afternoon meal. It has been a hot day.'

This was said with such slow authority that Ete Kamba thought that he really had cockroaches in his shorts. 'No, no sir, no cockroaches . . . only, em, only that, that, I might be late for Arit's party,' Ete Kamba blurted.

The sound of mocking laughter came from the inner room where the women were eating. It was from his mother. Ete Kamba recoiled like a frightened worm at the sound of it. So his mother too had been watching all that was going on in the front room. His father simply smiled and said, 'then hurry up, so that you won't be late for Arit's party.' He spat out the name Arit, as if it was a piece of offending chewing stick.

Ete Kamba knew that his family knew of his dislike for Arit. The girl was not popular in his family, and to come out, with what he had said must have seemed not only strange but funny to them. Mercifully, all went on eating to save his face. He knew his parents, they would not discuss it after he had gone, but each would be wondering what had come over him.

It was not difficult to know that something big was happening at Arit's place. Temporary shelter had been constructed and around it hung tiny flags of many colours. They looked so beautiful as they fluttered lazily in the wind. Before Ete Kamba turned the bushy corner that separated, his house from the opening that led to Arit's place, loud music floated to him. He hesitated. His insides worked from one level of emotion to the other. Should he turn round now and go back, just because he had been brought up to regard these loud happenings as repulsive. But was it really repulsive for one to be happy the only way one knew how to? Were his parents just a little jealous of Arit's parents? As far back as he could remember, Arit and her brother Philip had always had birthday parties as children. They were always smartly dressed and always had the air of people who had everything; yet their father was only a farmer, but a farmer with a difference. He could read and write and was able to get all the help the government could give. At one time all the people in Mankong would not buy his yams because they said he used so much fertilizer on his soil that the yams were wont to be overblown. At another time, he was bold enough to engage a young man doing his youth service to come and advise him on what to do. The young man did not stop at advice but brought in this huge thing, a kind of machine called a caterpillar. This worked for a week on his farm, much to the amusement of the children in the village and to the annoyance of the other farmers. Ete Kamba had since learnt that Arit's father had been right. If he were to be a farmer, he knew now that he would do even better. But to his parents, the Ekpeyong family were well known for dramatizing everything, even ordinary farming.

His family started feeling smug and a little proud when he gained an admission to his present school and Philip, Arit's brother did not even qualify for the entrance examination. 'Pride goeth before a fall,' his own father had judiciously said, when he heard of it. But what surprised Ete Kamba most was that his mother, who agreed with everything his father said, had got herself well-dressed the following Sunday and taken the trouble to offer an elaborate thanksgiving to God in the church making sure that it was well announced. She did not stop at that, she sought out Arit's mother and loudly sympathized with her for Philip's failure. Ete Kamba had been as confused as he was now on the rightness and wrongness of adults' behaviour. One thing he was sure of, his being at this party was going to be an added accolade to Arit's ego. But it was a chance between that or not seeing Nko again. He took a deep breath, made sure his shirt was nicely tucked in and that his sunglasses were well adjusted on his nose and walked confidently in.

'Ah, Nma, look who is coming to my party! Nma, come out and look.' Too late, Ete Kamba knew he was doomed.

Most of the well-dressed people at the party looked up and saw him. He almost missed a step, but managed to steady himself though his sunglasses suddenly felt loose. He was ushered in and given a chair by the side of a bench on which sat older men eating plates of jollof rice. The chair, a straight backed, plastic covered affair was shown to him as a mark of respect, no doubt. He was a person set apart, the future of the village of Mankong, the would-be elite and would-be man of importance. Well had he not gained an admission to an elitist grammar school?

The sun that afternoon was intense. The space in front of the Ekpeyong's house seemed to be oozing out heat. But for the celebrants the area would have been ghostly. It was that hot. Ete Kamba's shirt stuck to his body as he made vain attempts to wipe the sweat that was pouring from his forehead with his handkerchief. So preoccupied was he that the low voice near him made him aware of his immediate surrounding.

'Would you like beer or mineral with your rice?'

He looked up. It was Nko. He breathed a sigh of relief; she had not gone back to her village. His tortuous decision! to be present at Arit's noisy party had been worth it. He: forgot that he had just eaten. He smiled at Nko and replied, 'mineral, and thank you.'

He took the tray containing a plate heaped full with jollof rice and fried goat meat and forced himself to eat more than he required.

How could he live the rest of his life remembering the following four years after his first meeting with Nko? Those painful bitter-sweet years. Those four years that taught him so much about women, so much about Nko. How could he forget the exhilarating joy he felt the day he knew that there were people; many people in fact who did love others but could not express their love? In Nko's case he had thought that it was aloofness, but he soon realized that it was nothing, nothing at all, simply a kind of shyness. On discovering this he had felt secure. He had known her through and through; all he had to do was to work hard and then marry her one day. But that was not to be.

Tears, hot and salty, ballooned his eyes as the anger and frustration in his mind swelled and injected bitterness into his mouth. He banged his fist on the table in the library. Many readers looked at him angrily. The girl in red dress with the elaborate hairdo lowered her glasses, tut-tutted at his undignified display of emotion, stared at him, readjusting her glasses and carried on working.

'Sorry, so sorry.' Eta Kamba stammered lamely.

To get up would mean losing his place. The best step for him would have been to take a walk round the library building and then back, but something in him was enjoying remembering all that had passed. If he could bring himself to hate Nko enough, maybe he would have contemplated harming her. But no. What he felt for her now was a kind of contempt, and sometimes pity.

He remembered now, that he had almost burst his stomach that day over five years ago after eating a very rich meal of jollof rice atop his mother's simple soup with garri, all because it was served by Nko. He had sat there after the meal holding his painful belly, until mercifully, music started. Middle aged women, mostly friends of Arit's mother, took the floor. They kept shouting to the young ones to get up and dance. How could they? The amplifier was blaring and the women were singing throaty gospel songs and dancing to both. They soon got tired, and the young people heaved sighs of relief.

Arit had changed into another dress. She had changed her hairdo too. Ete Kamba wondered how she managed that. In the morning her hair had been straightened like that of Europeans, and then on top of that she had on a small hat, small enough to show her beautiful and glossy hair to better advantage. When he came there earlier on, her head was a mass of curls. Now she had something that looked like African raffia. She had plaited her hair on both sides of her head with a parting in the middle. This had been a common enough hair style, but Arit's looked so long and so black that Ete Kamba dug into his memory in an attempt to recall when her hair had ever been that long. It suited her though: she looked beautiful, only slightly strange. She now wore a yellow dress and was putting on a Mariamma record.

'Oh, come on let us dance,' she invited happily. Friends of her age group giggled nervously. Ete Kamba turned his eyes away.

'You don't need partners to dance, these days. In Aba we just dance singly.'

But when the music was almost halfway through and she noticed that if she did nothing her party was going to fall flat, she marched boldly towards Ete Kamba and pulled him from his chair. 'Come on, college boy, let us dance.'

Most of the adults watching started to clap. 'You see, women know what they want these days, they just go and get them. Not these old ones pretending, pretending ...' Ete Kamba heard Arit's father saying loudly. He felt like melting, but he went on dancing. And somehow after that, all the young people started to dance. The ice seemed to have melted miraculously. As soon as the second music started, he made a direct dive for Nko, before any other boy could get near her. She sat there for a split second, which to Ete Kamba seemed like eternity. For a while he thought she was going to refuse. This was a belated thought. He had been of the opinion that she would jump and be happy to dance with him, but now standing rather awkwardly in front of her, with everybody looking, and his heart thumping, he was not so sure. He was beginning to regret his impulsive move, as he watched the expression on Nko's face. The expression went from a blank innocent stare, to a demure near angry look, which was followed by that of resignation. She got up slowly and he tried to lead her rather proudly like a fisherman would lead a big catch, but Nko's arm though warm and soft, had' a tinge of stiffness. Ete Kamba let her arm be, and followed her into the centre of the fast filling dance floor.

She danced as if she hated the music. They did not touch each other, though many a time Ete Kamba felt like twisting and turning and showing her how much he was enjoying the music. He did a great deal of natural dancing with his friends on their free day in the dormitory. But now somehow he felt he had to control himself. He sensed that Nko would probably not like it. Oh, how in those early hours of their acquaintance he wished he could touch her, how he wished I hey could simply sit and talk and talk. But he reminded himself that Mankong was a small village. Word would get lo his parents immediately and he knew he would be reminded that he was a child of God. His heart sank when at the end of the music, Nko's mother called her away to serve rice to some newly arrived guests. He stood there slouching around, somehow refusing to sit down, and noticing that people around him were leaving him completely alone and not bothering to pressurize him to sit down. He followed Nko's busyness with the corners of his eyes, and when once he lifted his eyes and they met Arit's, he gave her such a scowl, that for once, confident Arit was beaten and quickly looked away. He waited for a very long time until Nko was free. This time he took his time and did not seem so eager, even though all the nerves in his body felt like dashing out for her. She still accepted him so slowly, but did not give the previous blank, near angry stare. If she had noticed that he did not dance with anybody else, she did not say. But this time he was rewarded with a ghost of a smile. Thus encouraged, he asked quickly, 'which school do you go to?'

'Methodist Central.'

'The one in Nbampka?'

Nko nodded and said yes, faintly.

Ete Kamba felt like shouting and saying, 'but that is a Secondary Grammar like mine, only that it is a mission school.' He would like her to be his friend, but suppose she were in a higher class? Impossible. She looked younger than he was, but he knew that looking young did not necessarily mean that one was young. He had never really thought seriously about the type of girls he would like to cultivate. He had belonged to that group of boys who were always on the periphery, watching other much more audacious boys making friends with girls and dropping them at will. He would giggle and make snide remarks, but nonetheless had always wondered how these clever beings managed to achieve so much. He would never admit to his mates that he was scared stiff though. The only time he thought about it, he had come to the conclusion that if he could not be bold enough to chat up a girl himself, he would get his parents to do it all for him when the time arrived. He never let it bother him, because he was ambitious. He wanted to further his education, and he knew that education was one of those preoccupations that demanded one's whole attention. And now that he had met Nko, he would like her to be younger than he was and to be in a lower grade at school. He would like all this very much; well, after seeing the way his parents lived, he would like to live like that. Not as poor perhaps, but with a woman who would be like his mother, but with this difference; she must be well educated. Yes, that was the type he would like. A very quiet and submissive woman, a good cook, a good listener, a good worker, a good mother with a good education to match. But her education must be a little less than his own, otherwise they would start talking on the same level. He was going to find out Nko's class. Another time maybe. Then something inside him, that part of us all which is always dormant and which we do not know we possess, and which has a way of showing itself when needed, maybe it is the survival instinct, maybe it is something else, yes that something was now taking up Ete Kamba's thinking and reminding him that he had better find out all he could about this girl otherwise he would either lose her or spend days, weeks, or even months worrying about whether she was in a higher class academically or not. That something seemed to be now speaking through him, that something now seemed to have this jaunty voice that was coming through his own shy mouth and boasting and saying, importantly, 'I am in my final year, soon I will have to try out my luck with our higher places of learning. Are you in your final year too?'

Nko gave the ghost of a smile he was now beginning to know and to expect. 'No, I am in my fourth year.' She said it so simply that Ete Kamba's previous pomposity stood out in both their senses.

Now that he had started, he might as well follow it up. He was now becoming surer of himself. At least she had two years to catch up with him. 'Gosh, you are a brain box.' This was meant to be both a patronizing and flattering statement.

'Not as brainy as you are. You won the scholarship, remember? My parents have to sweat out every kobo that goes into my education.'

The music stopped, and as he was about to start blaming himself for not making a definite date with her, it started again. It was a popular highlife number. The dancers did not have time to walk back to their seats. Ete Kamba did not want to ask her if she were tired, she could not be tired, she must not be. 'How did you know I won a scholarship?'

'Arit told us.' Nko said in her simple direct way.

He did not hold her as they danced, yet he felt he was floating unhinged in the air. At least they were dancing; at least she had talked to him; at least he had chatted up this girl all by himself. So he had the right to feel the way he was feeling, just as if he were in Seventh Heaven.

Ete Kamba's mind was still in this part of Heaven and he was so engrossed in being there, as his practised body moved naturally to the beat of the music, when Nko brought him down with, 'a big responsibility!'

'Yes,' he agreed, and then went on, 'Arit's career is not only going to be a big responsibility but judging from all that I have heard her say she could do with one's hair, I wonder whether the local women would be able to patronize her.'

Nko tossed and shook her scarf covered head, 'oh, but I was not referring to Arit, she'll be alright.'

'So what were you referring to?' He asked confidently.

'Our parents!'

'Ah, what about them? That we are a big responsibility to them?'

'No, they are our responsibility. They pay our fees, deny themselves so many thing that make life livable to see us go through this expensive education and when we've gone through it all, they are our responsibility.' This was followed by that smile which was particularly hers. She smiled with her eyes and at the same time stretched her lips in an innocent yet provocative way as if daring you to force her to show her teeth. But she did not need this provocativeness. Her cringing eyes said it all.

All Ete Kamba could do was to smile back, showing his teeth. It was getting too much for him. Not that he had thought that girls were brainless, only that for such an innocent looking girl like Nko to be capable of such deep convictions, and still manage to keep her apparent innocence, were things that were getting rather heavy, and with the beat of music too. And as if all that was not enough, she added another provocative thought by saying, 'especially when one is a girl'.

Ete Kamba nodded but was highly mystified. He did not know why ones parents should be such a heavy; responsibility. He loved his parents, yes. They were making sacrifices for his education, they were poor, but loved doing all they were doing, and his father, that wiry and hardworking farmer took so much pride in his little farm and had so much dignity in that small frame that was his body and sometimes talked as if he was sorry for the so called rich. He would have to help him in old age but he knew he would have to be subtle about it, otherwise that man would remind him that he had fed him all these years and never demanded anything from him. But all that was a long way away. His father was dry and skinny but it was difficult for Ete Kamba to begin to think of him as an old man. So Ete Kamba did not know the right comment to make on this, only to agree lamely with her, 'Yes, a big responsibility, especially when one is a girl.'

They did not have the opportunity of another dance, however, before she left to go to her mother, he had told her that he would write, that he would write through her school. Not that he wanted to do anything underhand, only he was sure that she would get his letter quicker that way.

As soon as she was called away, Ete Kamba looked about him and realized that apart from the square which Arit's parents had illuminated with fluorescent lights, darkness had descended in all its suddenness. Even the loud music could not still the determined night noises of so many little animals and insects. He had to go.

He went in and thanked Arit's parents. Arit was there, but did not acknowledge his presence. The parents thanked him politely for coming and also wished him well.

He left and followed the bush path that formed the partition between his part of the village and that of Arit. There was a song in his heart and there was music in his head. And for once he was able to thank God for a beautiful thanksgiving day. And then he added, as an afterthought 'and thank you God for all the Arits of this world, for without them how can one meet the hidden and secluded Nkos'.

He whistled his way home happily into the darkening night.

4. The First Letter

Ete Kamba remembered the sweet agony he went through for weeks after he had made that uncomfortable journey into the capital, Calabar, just to buy the writing paper and matching envelopes that he was going to use in writing Nko. He had sought through all the small shops in his village. All they yielded in the way of writing materials were either the horribly official looking khaki coloured envelopes and typing paper or the very white and plain ones. He was not going to use any of those for writing Nko. The trip to the capital would cost him almost a naira, but he did not care. He was able to earn the money easily by fetching and selling water when some of the taps in his village stopped running. This was something of a daily occurrence - water not running in one part of the village, but running in another part. He made several trips and was able to earn three naira. With this he made his trip to the capital.

He had set out from his village in one of his best trousers. But the day was wet and sloshy and before he had walked the one and a half kilometres it took to reach the main road, he was plastered with mud. It threatened to rain all the time, but he kept praying that it would not degenerate into a heavy downpour, the type that is well known in that part of the country. He stood by the side of the road and thumbed and waved and cursed at so many taxis and private cars, yet they all kept speeding by. He was beginning to despair, when a man on a motorcycle stopped. It would only cost him half the price to the market in Calabar. Ete Kamba looked down at his trousers and saw the state of his shoes. He looked up at the sky and was rewarded with the sight of angry clouds fast forming and on the verge of letting out bucketfuls of rain, then he knew that he had to accept the offer. The man gave him the spare helmet and he sat behind him. He hooted off with the wind stinging his eyes and rushing through their bodies. Ete Kamba was beginning to feel a little chill in his damp shirt when he saw that they were already in Murtala Highway. They were nearing the market.

A police officer stopped them to check the bundles the owner of the scooter was carrying. The man protested that they were only his overnight clothes. But the officer was adamant.

'A say a won see am,' he glowered.

The owner of the scooter felt disgraced after the officer had exposed to the public his old work clothes, all tattered and dirty. The man was probably a palm wine tapper or a grave digger or something, but whatever it was, he was not proud of his job.

'These p'lice men, na rogue, rogue.'

'Maybe him wan dash', Ete Kamba supplied.

'You tink a no know dat! Dis kontiri, disi kontiri, my broder, nawar!'

They could not go on to talk about the country in depth because they had commenced their journey. The traffic was not only heavy, but reckless as well. Cars and taxis were coming in from all sides; this one was hooting and that was cursing, but the man and his motor cycle, with Ete Kamba behind him, manoeuvred in between them all. They soon neared the market. The motor bike owner stopped and demanded his money. Ete Kamba gave him a naira, but the man said he had no change. The situation was almost deadlock. Ete Kamba then made a suggestion: 'I will go into the post office to buy some stamps. I am sure they have change there.'

The motorbike man held his chin and speculated. He made a 'hmmmmm' sound and then said, dipping his hand into the front of his trouser pocket, 'look, a get fifty kobo change. Why you no share the loss. A gee you fifty kobo and you gee me a naira'. He finished smiling broadly.

So that was it, Ete Kamba thought. The man charged him only twenty five kobo, but he wanted to use the same opportunity to claim double the amount. Ete Kamba had to smile at the cleverness of men like the motorbike owner. First this one had used his scooter as a taxi, and now this. He would have given in, and let him have his way simply for the fun of it, after all twenty five kobo would not kill him, but he worked very hard for his money too - fetching and carrying water. So in his forthright way he told the motorbike man how he got his money.

'Na true?' The man asked, incredulity spreading all over his sweaty face. 'I bin tink say you be rich man pikin, rich college boy.'

Ete Kamba shook his head. He was a farmer's son, a college boy yes, but definitely not a rich man's son.

Miraculously, the correct change came tumbling out. Ete Kamba was like one in a daze. The man hurried, snatched the naira note from him, shook his hand, adjusted his helmet and hooted his way into the crowded part of the market. Ete Kamba shook himself, to make sure he was not dreaming. Was the man being dishonest or not? Who authorized the likes of him to become Robin Hoods of Calabar? Ete Kamba could find no answer. He shook his head, half walked and half pushed himself towards the centre of the market, where it would be easier to cross to the other side of the road in search of the bookstalls he knew were situated there. Then he was faced with the almost impossible job of trying to cross from one side of the biggest market in Calabar to the other.

When you enter into the middle of the market in Calabar, you find a policeman occupying a position of eminence in the centre. He, in his orange shirt, black trousers and black hat, flails the in-coming and the out-going traffic with his hands. A road comes from his right, another from his left, one from his back, and the other from his front all culminating in the centre where he stood - a diminutive man performing a herculean job.

He was very artistic in his duties, that Calabar policeman. He would swing this way and that, to the music playing in his head. He would stretch out one arm and curve the other, his fingers tapping the air - an adept musical conductor, conducting a familiar orchestra completely immune to all the orchestrated applause coming from his audience; so complete, so happy was he in his own performance. At the commencement of the air tapping, all hell would be let loose. Taxis, motor bikes, cycles on both sides would roar into action, whilst the ones in front and at his back would be hooting and making frantic signs for him to hurry up and wave their sides on. But those in action would go at such a breakneck speed, that one would have thought that this was a car racing competition. Impatient taxis in their yellow colouring with a splash of blue in the middle would meander in between the cars in a hurry to get on first. One sometimes wondered where they wanted to get to in such a hurry. As the policeman swung to the other side, and commenced his wind tapping and arm flailing, the first side would stop with brakes screeching and angry drivers shouting rude things to the driver right in front of them. Most drivers were sure that but for the slow person in front, they would have sped through before the police officer changed his direction. The same process would now repeat itself, only this time it would be the other way.

Ete Kamba stood on one side after the motorbike rider had left him, trying to work out how he was going to cross to the other side where he knew the stalls were. He wondered as he stood there whether it was a sensible thing to have the busiest road in town going through the town's busiest market. He knew that the idea of moving the market from its present position was fast becoming a political issue, in which the owners of the town maintained that the market had always been there and that nothing but an earthquake would shift it. As no politician would like to be voted out of office, they all pledged to keep the market where it had always been. But if that was the case, then, they could move the roads. He was surprised that there were not more deaths than the few hundreds recorded around this place every year. Or was this the only way those clever politicians could think of controlling the population? Attract more people to places of greater risks, then of course there would be more deaths. Maybe so. But he was determined not to be one of the casualties. So he waited patiently.

A group of women who saw him standing there stood beside him. They were incessantly being forced to shift their position by this cyclist and that taxi driver, as there were no elevated sidewalks for pedestrians, since that particular road was so narrow. The planners never realized that Calabar would grow so fast, and Nigeria as a whole so rich overnight that there would be so many families with so many cars; that it would be almost impossible for people to walk. A sane middle class Nigerian would rather be seen dead than walk along the main road. Walking was now an occupation for the very poor. That, in a way was not a bad thing. Because now it meant the rich fat ones would die off quickly. They were doing so already - sending themselves to untimely graves with hypertension mainly, because of exposure to so many unnecessary hours in traffic jams. Ete Kamba wished he were in a powerful position. He would have banned all cars from public places, would expand the roads so that people could walk. 'Ete Kamba, you are not in a position of power yet. Your immediate problem is to cross this road,' he said to himself in silent admonishment.

He looked around and saw to his amusement that the few people around him had grown into a crowd - a crowd that was now very noisy and becoming a force to be reckoned with. Cyclists could no longer confuse them with their bell ringing. And the taxis were booed. Then, one private car owner, at the great risk of having his white, Nigerian-assembled Peugeot car smashed on him from the rear, waved his arms erratically to warn the car behind him that he was stopping. The crowd shouted with joy. Some women blessed him, telling him that he would not die in his car, others called him a God-fearing person and hoped he would live to see his grandchildren's children. But the taxi man behind him called him the stupid idiotic son of the devil. The legend in front of the taxi said, 'Jesus saves.'

Ete Kamba did not miss this golden opportunity. He crossed over quickly to the other side of this death trap. 'Whew!' he gasped, Nigeria and her population. 'Well', he rationalized as he shrugged his young shoulders, 'this is progress.'

There was a long narrow gap between the soap powder sellers and those that sold imported foodstuffs. The gap was so narrow that one would have to wait whenever another person was coming from the opposite side. It was even more complicated now because it had been raining. Many a time, he practically had to step into somebody's stall causing the owner to ask eagerly if he wanted something. He had to apologize saying that he was only looking for the bookstalls.

'Na down dere.'

The 'down there', seemed so far away, but he eventually got there. He was lucky also in that he found a rich looking writing paper with matching envelopes, just the type he had wanted to write Nko with. He bought a packet of envelopes and another of writing paper. So sure was he of writing many, many letters to Nko. As he did not go to Calabar often, he sought and bought his mother a tin of corned beef and a small packet of soap. He smiled as he

visualized the happiness that would radiate on his
mother's face when she saw what he bought her from
Calabar. Luckily he had enough change in his pocket
to buy himself a cold bottle of Dr Pepper mineral and
a packet of groundnuts. Having thus refreshed
himself, he boarded a coach on its way to Lagos. It
stopped for him to come down off the main road
leading to his village.

That night, by the hurricane lamp, with sweet
music in his head, and youthful hopefulness
pounding in his heart, he penned his first love letter
to his first adult love. Ete Kamba was growing into a
man.

He had actually laboured, in copying and
recopying his letter to her. He used all the sweet
romantic words he had gathered from the abundant
cheap penny dreadfuls he had bought and read from
Calabar market. He was quite sure that Nko would be
'thrilled to pieces' on receiving such a letter. She
would reply straightaway telling him in equally
flamboyant terms, how much she loved him, and
how she had been waiting all her sixteen years of life
for just a man like him. For had his mother not told
him continually that 'one lucky woman would get
you one day?' Yet, six weeks later, Nko had not
bothered to reply. And Ete Kamba was hurt.

He was so shocked and began to wonder about
his mother's estimation of him for once. His mother,
to him, had been the epitome of womanhood, the
type whose price was above the biblical rubies. The
type who took pride not in herself but in her man.
The type who would always obey her man, no matter
what, even if he commanded her to walk through fire,

the type that never questioned. He had thought all women were like that, and should be like that. Were some women different then? Was his mother becoming one of the older generation? Or was she just filling his head with all these nice words simply because he was her son and she loved and adored him, and had the fact that he seemed to be cut out for an elitist adulthood heightened her pride in him? But blast it all, one never marries one's mother! It's never done. He would have to go out, to face the new woman, try to understand her and maybe get a partner and friend for himself. Many a time he felt like relieving himself and talking all these things out with his best friends, Ikem and Akpan. After all, these boys had talked to him about their numerous escapades with women and had even boasted about their ideas of the town's richest and most notorious female models. They had all laughed and made stupid remarks about such girls and loose women. He feared his friends might relegate Nko to that level. And he did not like that. Nko was private. The pain she was dealing out to him was private, the type of bittersweet pain that one loathed to share with another, however close. So, for weeks, Ete Kamba thought he was alone in carrying the heaviness with him.

He soon realized that he was wrong in thinking that his pain was private when he asked the junior boy, Effiong, whose duty it was to collect letters, for the umpteenth time whether there was any letter for him. The boy's reply was the same. 'No sir, no letter for you today.' This was beginning to sound like a song.

'Expecting a letter from her then?' asked Ikem, that tall, observant Ibo boy with exaggerated behaviour.

Ete Kamba smiled and replied, 'no', unconvincingly.

'So there you are, our Adam. You have been deceived by Eve. She has given you the forbidden apple to eat and you have enjoyed it and now she is taunting you with it. Boy, when did it happen? During the vacation? You are a dark horse, Ete...'

'Yeah, and you don't even eat properly.' Akpan butted in as usual, uninvited. 'Now that you have tasted evil you have no appetite for ordinary food. According to the Scriptures, you should be ashamed of yourself and hide, not parade your woes.'

'No, he is shrinking from us like Adam, because he is guilty.'

'I warned him, nobody can blame me for not doing my bit. I did warn him.' Ikem finalized, and this statement was greeted by a burst of unreserved laughter.

Ete Kamba knew then that they had suspected. He also knew better than to lose his temper, but he would have liked to give Ikem a big blow on both his shiny cheeks. Instead, he smiled mildly whilst the fires in his eyes spoke volumes. And somehow, his friends' laughter died as abruptly as it had started. They guessed that their friend was not going to share this one with them. 'It's no joke.' And somehow, according to that unwritten law which emerges at some unspeakable time from among young adult students, they knew they had to respect his feelings.

Ete Kamba hated himself for being so transparent.

But however closely his friends tried to tease him about Nko, he now refused to discuss her. Thus for the first time in his life he was being forced to be distanced from his friends. Yes, Ikem was right, now he felt like the proverbial Adam, who had shrunk away from God after eating the apple. Now he shrank from his friends.

And then after he had completely given up hope, a miracle, or near miracle happened. How he remembered that day clearly. The same first year, tottered up, panting doglike to him, as they were about to commence the much hated cross country race. They all hated this strength sapping exercise, but it was a discipline which every student had to go through. His heart beat very fast when he heard what little Effiong had to say.

'A letter sir, a letter has arrived sir. It is for you, the letter!' Effiong gasped.

He saw that the stupid boy did not bring the letter with him but had left it in his cubicle in the dormitory. And the distance between the dormitory and the gymnasium in which they were all getting ready for the race was about half a kilometre. It would look stupid for him to avoid the race just because of the letter. It might not even be *the* letter, or had little Effiong opened it? He peered closely at the little boy whose height was barely above his waist and wondered how he knew that it was the letter he had been expecting. Maybe Nko had replied to him in an equally expensive blue envelope, the very loud type he had used. To think that these first-years were not as innocent as they pretended to be. He caught Effiong's eyes, and a ghost of mischievous smile spread across his young impish face. He screwed his eyes at his prefect and house captain and stood with his bandy legs apart and demanded wordlessly, 'what now? Aren't you going to say thank you to me, you love sick fool?'

But there was one thing Ete Kamba was not going to show and that was any obvious signs of weakness. His friends could have guessed what he was going through, but he was going to leave it like that to keep them guessing. He was not going to confirm their doubts. So he summoned up his cool prefect voice and said, 'thank you Effiong,' and then demanded sharply, 'but why aren't you running?'

The screwed mischievous near grin evaporated from the face of the cub student. He became serious, almost to the point of standing straight and correcting the bandiness of his tiny legs. 'I have malaria, sir,' he stammered.

'Ah, I see, but make sure you are better next Wednesday,' Ete Kamba replied, feigning seriousness, yet unable to cover the kindly gleam in his eyes.

'Yessir, thank you sir!' Effiong ran back to the dormitory.

'For somebody who has malaria, he is not doing too badly with those bandy legs of his.' Ikem felt confident enough to remark. He too had seen the gleam in Ete Kamba's eyes.

'Remember your first year, Ikem, or have you forgotten so soon?'

They both laughed so richly. They had all done it before - dodging the Wednesday cross country race.

Ete Kamba could now not remember how he survived that morning's cross country. But somehow he did. He took the trouble to put on an elaborate air of calmness and absent-mindedness, to the point that Ikem, who did not miss a thing, had to remark rather casually, 'to think that you have been dying for this letter, and now that you know it is here, you are ostentatiously in no hurry to read it.'

'Have you not heard what they say, that there is more excitement in chasing than in actually getting.' Akpan, as philosophical as ever, put in.

'Look, how do you know it is from her anyway?' Ete Kamba countered voicing aloud his fears.

'Oh, so it's a her. A female! I thought we were being made to understand that such a person did not exist for you and that all this mooning and your lack of appetite were because you were at last shedding off your adolescence and growing into a man.' Ikem joked.

He had given himself away. And he had to smile despite his inner turmoil. He saw the celebrated letter. The sight of it made him feel like a deflated balloon. It was in a white envelope, clean yes, but just plain white envelope with nothing at its back to tell him or anybody who the writer was. It could have been from anybody, only he himself should know that it was from Nko. The handwriting was tiny, it was light, it was a woman's, but he was determined to bluff his inquisitive friends off. A mixture of anger and disappointment worked inside him. He was now beginning to hate school boarding house life. Gosh, he needed his privacy so.

'Is it from her?' A voice shouted at him from the other side of the room.

'Sh sh sh,' came another voice in an elaborate stage whisper. 'He is in deep meditation.'

Then Ete Kamba snapped. 'Oh, for God's sake, be sensible. What sane girlfriend would write to her lover in a white envelope without her name at the back? Please, sirs, do be sensible. Why has an ordinary letter become so important; what of your own letters, open yours.' Ete Kamba cried, hating himself all the while for failing to control his emotion.

'I know the type of girl who would do exactly that, the very modern and educated girl, probably in a mission school. Could even be a nun. Those sets are really snakes but exciting.' Ikem would always find something to say.

Ete Kamba ignored him. They all saw that he wanted to read his letter at leisure and maybe in privacy. So Akpan made an elaborate show of changing the subject much to the disappointment of Ikem and a few others. Akpan succeeded, and Ete Kamba was grateful.

The letter itself did not say much, only to apologize for the delay. It had an air of humility, and at the same time showed the writer as somebody who would never be pushed into saying everything she felt. She was glad to have been Chosen to be his friend. And she would like him to be hers. But they were both busy. Their future was much more important, for were they not responsible to their parents and to their country, Nigeria? She would love to receive his letters whenever he had time to write but if he were busy, she would understand. She wished him luck in his forthcoming entrance examination to the university, and she was sincerely his, Nko.

Ete Kamba's first reaction was humiliation. To

think that he had made that journey to Calabar, that he had racked his brains in search of the most endearing terms he could think of, all with which to write Nko. And his reward, a reply on a plain paper and in a language that would befit a nun. Doubts crept into his mind. There are as they say many fishes in the river. He was not sure he had the patience to play with a girl who was going to play at being hard to get. Nko was right. He had to concentrate on getting a place in the university. When there, he was sure of getting as many modern and even beautiful girls as he wanted. He had heard that Nigerian university girls don't usually find husbands, and would jump at any male student who showed interest in their direction. That was a pity, because he really thought he would have learnt to love Nko. But he was not made to be tortured by a woman.

He went to bed that night a much more mature young man. He lay there flat on his back listening and feeling sympathy with a nearby frog who was calling its mate. The noise soon stopped, the frog had found its mate, and all was silence. Ete Kamba sighed and drifted into sleep, thinking - 'at least, she replied to my letter.'

5. Adult's Problem

Then came one of the most puzzling days of all.

It was a Friday dawn. There was that lethargic feeling of the weekend approach. For once it was not raining and the sun that rose was bright and mildly warm. The air was humid. There were plenty of puddles and mud all along the untarred bits of the road. Since it was the season of heavy rainfall, the tarred roads had developed gaping holes in many places. The leaves on the trees hung limp, even the threadlike ones of giant whistling plants hung low, drooping with the weight of the water that had been pouring on them for days: there they were now, those suffering spidery leaves waiting and ready like patient animals for the next downpour which they knew would only be an hour or so away. This part of the world has been over blessed with plentiful rainfall.

For the past week, Ete Kamba had plunged into a moodiness almost akin to depression. He was scared. He had to make a decision on what to do now that he had finished his schooling. He had killed his waiting time by going daily to the farm with his father. The old man was at first puzzled about this, but after a while gave in and allowed him to come. He had thought that such a demeaning job like farming was not for the likes of his son who had not only passed his school certificate exams but had taken an entrance examination to their one and only University of Calabar. So he had let him be. He had even come to appreciate his help and was getting used to it.

For Ete Kamba it was a way of working out his fear. If all failed and he could not gain a scholarship admission, he would have to break it gently to his parents, that he would consider going into the teaching profession. He would like to study further and maybe do a retake for the entrance, but all this he could combine with a teaching job, as the long holidays would offer him the opportunity to study.

Ete Kamba knew that on this Friday morning, he would have to summon up courage and go up to Calabar to face the music. He had refused breakfast, and as usual thought he was hiding his anxiety and secrets well. But his parents knew and watched him as it were from a distance. He rolled over on his bed, looking vacantly towards the door.

'You are not going to the farm with me today?' It was his father's voice, asking falteringly. Ete Kamba could hear him chewing his early morning kolanut meditatively as he walked about the other room getting this and that.

'No, father. I am sorry.'

'I understand, son. Don't let it weigh you down. Tell us about it, when you feel you can talk.'

'Yes, father, have a nice day.'

'Thank you, son. I will.'

He heard his father leave, and knew his silent mother had gone to her cassava patch. He also knew that even though he had refused breakfast, she would leave him something to eat in case he had a change of mind. Mechanically he got up, washed himself and got ready to leave for Calabar. He knew the results must have been out since Monday, but those of them in the remote villages would rather wait until the end of the week. He made his trip to Calabar like one in a daze, letting the atmosphere pass through him, and not taking any in. He thought it was cruel to ask would-be students to come to the campus for their results. Those who organized these things did not take into consideration how students would feel if they failed to make it. Thoughtless fools!

When in the bus, he noticed with relief that he was not the only passenger going to the university. The mammy lorry lumbered into Calabar and dropped them off in the Motor Park at the corner of Lagos Road.

To get to the university, one had to walk for a few minutes outside the market. Then you would stand by the road, and you would shout at one of the yellow vehicles with the blue horizontal lines running all round it like a belt. Most of them were Peugeot cars, with the word 'taxi' written in different styles, depending on the whim of the owner. Nearly all of them had legends like, 'I am a miracle' and 'Do you love Jesus' and many such religious slogans. Calabar is one of those places where a modern African brand of religion is mushrooming fast.

Ete Kamba now knew for sure that the other three young men walking with him away from the Motor Park to the corner road were going to the same place as him. They hailed taxi after taxi, calling Unical after them. One eventually stopped and they all got in. No one dared talk. The air was heavy with that kind of suspense that seemed to be breathing, and very much alive. Ete Kamba thought he was nervous, but he seemed to be faring so much better than the jumpy young man sitting next to him and eating away at all his fingernails and would soon progress to eating his fingers too. Ete Kamba looked at him: he was a lanky, narrow faced boy with worried eyes that roamed. Ete Kamba did not want to look at him again. He had enough worries of his own.

He paid his fare and half ran and half walked to the gates of the university. The wall built around the university campus was painted cream. But the top ends were done in pale blue. The iron gate that now stood wide open was done in the contrasting colour, pale blue. To the right of the big gate was the tiny hut-like structure with security written on it in black letters. Ete Kamba had thought that he would be questioned by one of the black uniformed men with strange looking caps that stood about listlessly watching the comings and goings. One of them was flagging and waving on the in and out going traffic. Ete Kamba hesitated for a while. Then came this shout:

'Ete! Ete Kamba, Ete! You are in, you lucky devil. You are in! Yes, in and with a scholarship too!'

Ete Kamba turned, and saw Akpan coming, trying to do some kind of funny slow fox trot at the same time. He held Ete Kamba and they both capered shamelessly for a while, much to the amusement of so many others standing by - a mixed crowd of people, some happy at their results others rooted to the spot with the shock of failure. Sweat of joy poured from the heads of the two young men. They soon had to stop dancing simply because other new people were coming in and reading their own good results too. Ete Kamba and Akpan's happiness were being eclipsed by those of others. It was not until then that Ete Kamba remembered that he had not even seen the results himself. Then he stopped, like somebody just woken from a dream, he gasped, 'you could have made a mistake.'

'Yes I could have, only that as far as I know, there is only one Ete Kamba who went to the States Grammar. You are frightened and unsure, but why argue, let's go and see.' A slow mocking smile spread over his moon shaped face. 'It's nice to see one's name in print.'

'It depends in which print the name is. If one's name is among the list of failures, you won't like that would you?' Ete Kamba sounded morbid. Fear was creeping into him again.

Akpan laughed loud, his little mouth seemed to have acquired extra width. They went to the board together, and right there under the 'Scholarship' heading, Ete Kamba saw his name.

'Now you see it?' Akpan asked.

'Now I see it, but where is yours, my friend?'

'Right there, not clever enough for a scholarship, but this body is happy to find its name under this list and not there,' he said pointing to the other board on which there was another long list, this time of failures.

Ete Kamba smiled mildly, patted his school friend on the back and said, 'well done!' He knew though that he had to curb his exuberance.

Somehow they got home: Akpan went to his parents and Ete Kamba to his. Ete Kamba could not tell for sure how that evening started, matured and then ended up the way it did. First in a joyous daze, he felt his mother cuddling him, then his father patting his back; his sisters and brothers dancing around him. There were people and neighbours, friends, and then it led to a party - one that looked impromptu and yet had a touch of calculation.

Until that very evening Ete Kamba thought that he hated showy noisy gatherings. He had it that night, he had to face it first reluctantly. Then a thought came to him - rarely does a person gain such a prestigious admission into such a university twice in one's life. And looking at the happiness on the faces of the rest of the members of his family, he felt justified in being happy and showy too. His mother would not have it otherwise anyway. The older men sat around his father, who had miraculously managed to procure several jerry cans full of palm wine. They sat there drinking and talking and eating kolanuts and goat meat. How did his family manage to get all these delicacies? Did they know beforehand that he would pass? Had somebody been to Calabar before him ? This party looked so planned.

The young set was even livelier. Arit and her brother Philip came, carrying bottles of mineral, soft drinks and their father donated a case of Champion beer. Arit came to him and said, 'Ete Kamba, thank you for putting our little village on the map of the knowledged.' He was so overcome that very unlike him, he kissed her on the cheek. She laughed, but he noticed that though she tried to make her laughter light-hearted and silly, Arit was trying to cover up her more serious personality. From that evening, Ete Kamba stopped taking Arit for granted and looking down on her. He sensed that her superficialities notwithstanding, she was capable of deep thinking.

His eyes were still following her, when he felt a gentle tap on his shoulder and turned.

'Congratulations Ete, you have done us proud.' It was Nko.

'How the hell did you know? To come all this way in a matter of minutes?'

Nko laughed out loud - a thing of rarity. She showed part of her teeth, another miraculous feat. So many strange and baffling things were happening this night.

'I say, how did you know? How come you had the courage to come to our house uninvited and how come you have the pluck to step up to me and stand there... ?'

He stopped asking questions as he saw that Nko went quickly back to her thin smile. Her eyes were dancing though. She was happy and amused and again for once she was allowing it to show. 'Aren't you happy to see so many of your friends here tonight, including me?'

'Yes, yes, I am happy and grateful, maybe too grateful. It's just that...'

She cut in, 'Don't worry, just leave it like that, and once more congratulations,'

Ete Kamba held her hand, and he somehow had that uncanny feeling that comes to us all when we suspect that somebody is watching us rather too closely, too embarrassingly closely. He turned his head abruptly. Too abruptly for his mother, who was carrying a calabash of kolanuts and disappearing into their modest house. Their eyes had met, and he thought he saw her nod, very, very slightly, almost like a bow, yes, an assenting nod. 'Whew!' he breathed, 'women are not always what they seem, even mother.'

'I do beg your pardon,' Nko asked, not too gently.

Ete Kamba simply laughed and led her to her seat.

The party went into its fullest swing. He danced with all the local girls present, but had many, many dances with Nko. During one of them Nko remarked, 'I always knew you would go through, but your mother would not believe me. We were all worried when you were so moody, but I told myself; "he will get it, he will get the scholarship. If there is only one being awarded, it should go to Ete Kamba."'

'But you all knew I passed before today?'

Nko nodded.

'Even my father?'

'I should think so, is he not a human being?'

'It's just that, well I thought, no I am beginning to think that this type of thing is a woman's game.'

'What game?' Nko asked her eyes dancing once more.

'Never mind, I am not quite clear of it myself.'

It was getting late, and people started drifting home. Ete Kamba went to Nko who was talking to her cousin Arit, and asked, 'how are you going to get home?'

'You mean to Nbamkpa, tonight? Oh, Ete Kamba, for God's sake wake up,' laughed Arit.

'I am staying the weekend with Arit, and would also like to attend the Thanksgiving service for your success on Sunday.'

'Oh, Thanksgiving! Is there going to be one? In that case Arit, I would like to talk to Nko, then I will bring her to your place.'

'I don't know whether we can leave her with you,' Arit began. But her brother Philip strolled over and said lightly: 'Oh for God's sake, Arit. Nko is a young woman of eighteen, not an eight-year-old.'

'But she is our guest.'

'That's true, sister, but if you ask me, I would say she came here to Mankong just for this. Have fun, old boy. Come, sister, let's go home now!'

Nko and Ete Kamba watched as Philip jokingly half pulled his sister Arit with him away into the darkening night.

When all had gone, they sat on a bench on the veranda in front of Ete Kamba's house and talked. Or it was better to say that he talked and she listened. The night soon deepened and he knew that it was time to take her through the riot of entangled tropical growth that demarcated his part of the village from that of her cousin's. It would look malevolently darker and deeper tonight because there was no moon. Tiny distant stars tried to lighten the atmosphere; here and there the earthly fire flies were doing their share - opening and closing at will - but so determined was the night to be mysterious that though the forest was sleepless, there was still an unmistakable stillness.

If you walked a few paces from Ete Kamba's house, you would pass the thatched one belonging to Ekpeyong the shoe maker. Ekpeyong was not a poor man, for his children played about with their noisy colourful tricycles and real imported footballs. But he refused, or maybe it was better to say that he did not want, his house covered in corrugated iron sheets like the ones Ete Kamba's parents had. Mind you, on hot afternoons, when everything seemed so still, clammy and sluggish, the Ekpeyong's house was always cool, whilst the ones belonging to his neighbours were more like ovens.

Next to the Ekpeyong's house was this half built house. It had always been like that, unfinished, since Ete Kamba could remember. The owner, who they say lived in the country's capital of Lagos, had used that building to lay claim to that piece of land. He did not roof the house and he did not demolish it. It was just there, standing there open to the sky, without a head. Inside however, was a riotous jungle of creeping plants and thick undergrowth.

Ete Kamba took Nko's hand, led her through the path that ran by the side of the house. The thought of what he was going to do or what he was expected to do did not at all cross his mind. He simply led, and she followed as it were into nowhere.

Then suddenly he turned round, and just then a pale star fit up his face and Nko was able to see that it was distorted by another force - anger, thirst or maybe desire - she was not given time to find out. He bore on her, unceremoniously half pushed and half dragged her towards the walls of this unfinished house, then right to a corner inside. He was determined. He had squared his shoulders ready to combat any protest, but none came. For once Nko allowed him to touch, to fondle and to know her. She allowed him, she gave in, and she gave him all, her body yielding, responding to his demands, his thirst, his hunger. He became lightheaded; he became light fingered; he surprised Nko; he surprised himself. She was exhilarating, she was a bundle of soft tender, warm flesh, very young, very moist, not very difficult. They stayed there for a very long time, until she started to wilt. Her legs became weak. Ete Kamba sighed, gave her one of his now fast becoming familiar, long, near crumbling kisses, and unwillingly led her slowly out of the corner of the unfinished house into the dark open, then led her, weak and slightly shaken to her cousin's house. Their goodbyes were tiny little whispers.

He, beleaguered by myriads of confusing thoughts, pigeon stepped his way back, not bothering to use the torch he was holding to light his way. 'What have we done? What have I done? Oh my God, was this planned to be so?'

Dazed, he crept into his home careful not to wake his sleeping family. Then suddenly a low guttural voice came from the darkness, 'are you back, son?'

'Yes, father, have you not gone to sleep yet?' He had a big task in keeping his voice even. He wanted to be by himself.

This was one of those times he did not want to talk not even to his great chum, his father.

'My son, I am so happy today. Congratulations, son.' Then came that mischievous twitter his father usually gave him when they shared a joke on the farm, as he added; 'I am sure she was warm and yielding. Lucky girl, with a young man like you, her future is secured. Women love security,' he finished darkly.

Before Ete Kamba could recover and maybe tell his father to mind his own business, that man had impatiently walked in, into that part of the house that belonged to him and Ete Kamba's mother. His back was proud, still and unyielding, as if taunting his son, daring him to enter with him. Ete Kamba looked at him malevolently, that tiny man, his father, going in to his mother, and he looked back in his mind's eye, to the human warmth and tenderness he had just experienced, and muttered angrily, 'Crafty old devil, lucky one as well.' He knew his mother would be there waiting, full of useless questions about him, and his father would assure her in his tongue-tied grunty way that he was all right. They would calm, assure and pacify each other in their human closeness, sealing up their very own little secrets, secrets which even he, a much loved son had no right to share. He had to look for his own path.

He dropped himself on his own bachelor's bed. For a while he tossed this way and that, very restless. Such a baffling confusing day. When he woke this morning, he had no idea the day was going to be so full. Now at the end of it, he knew his future was secured as long as he worked hard at his studies in English and Linguistics at his State University of Calabar. He now knew Nko, that elusive and rather unapproachable girl; she now suddenly seemed to be there, within his reach, waiting for him, simply waiting for him to take her. She still had that nun's remote look, but somehow for no reason he could fathom, he was disappointed.

Somehow she had brought added happiness to this day, and somehow taken it all away, leaving him with confusion and baffled resentments. It was an anti-climax. He wished Nko had not allowed him to do it. Not on a day like this. He wished it had not happened. It had made it all look as if she was only waiting for him to be a successful person. Yet somehow he was happy as well. But wait a minute, was Nko a virgin? Was that what had been worrying him? All those long talks and books he had read about deflowering an innocent girl. He could not say for sure, because he did not know. Stupid him, he did not check. They did it backing the wall. Did he find her difficult to penetrate? He could not tell. He had forgotten, and he did not notice. They were so carried away. But what right had she got to be carried away? She was supposed to be in pain. That was what his friends had said. Was it because they did it by the wall?

Yes, by the wall. He took his torch, sneaked out of the house. There was only one way to find out. He saw the area where they had trampled in their frenzy, his lighted torch poured into every hole and every corner, he even searched the blades of every leaf, looking this way and that, his heart pounding. He hoped to marry Nko someday, but tonight he was desperate for that blood she ought to have shed. He went round the place over and over again, until he could feel from the night's air, that morning was not too far away.

Had Nko played a trick on him? Was all that nun and remote little-girl-lost look an armour of deception? Maybe he did not penetrate. That must be it. His father had said to him, 'I hope she was warm and yielding.' The old man did not mean his going all the way, he only meant light fondling and at worst heavy petting. He knew his son Ete Kamba would not be so stupid as to go all the way with a girl he knew they had all approved of. No, he couldn't have. Nko would not have allowed it. But he had let out warm pressing spurts of his seed inside her. He had felt it, when they were coming and when he released them unable to hold on any longer. He had felt her shiver, and wilt. It had happened, or maybe miraculously it did not happen. Maybe she was still intact. He wanted a virgin, an educated virgin, nice wholesome unspoilt for his bride when he qualified. And a virgin he was going to have. He would ask his father, he ought to know.

He came near the door that led to his parents' room. And then he heard it - his mother's voice, that silly woman was laughing quietly in a sickly sort of way, and wait a minute, she was calling his father. What? Calling him her tiger? Tiger! Good Lord!

Ete Kamba rushed like a blindfolded person into his room. The noise woke the whole house. He heard his father asking what it was. He had kept quiet, standing at ease, remaining still, letting his mind wander. He was to remember this day, especially this night for years and years. He would have to ponder over it, dream about it, wake up at night and go through it in detail trying to piece it all together again in an attempt to find out what he was looking for.

His feeling of initial joy had become that of compromise, and then of near bitterness, but not of full disappointment. He calmed himself as the house grew quiet once more. In a way he was grateful that this day had happened. It was one of those incidents that simply just happened, even though one did not go out of one's way to make it so, but when it happened, one was grateful that one had allowed it to. Ete Kamba was calmer and an air of adult responsibility swept over him. At twenty he realized that he had seen, and experienced a near full adult's life. He was a man, and as a man, he would have to find his own pathway. And when he had found it, he was going to be responsible for it.

He must learn to leave his parents alone. His problems were now with his future, and his future included Nko. But was Nko a virgin, or was she still one?

6. Quest for Virginity

'You are not a virgin, are you?' This was such an abrupt question that the strangeness of it sounded even stranger in the ears of the questioner, Ete Kamba.

They were in his room at the university. He had been lucky to have this room to himself, before the arrival of the other students. Nko had come with him, she had helped him in putting his things in the right places, and was about to tell him that she had to go home.

Ete Kamba saw her despair after his untoward question. She had wilted like a tender flower that had been molested by a strong wind. It was momentary though. She stood up, her head high, but eyes still alluringly down, breathing deeply - that scarf he hated and had come to regard as part of her, was still there tightly tied around her head. Her young breasts stood out against her thin blouse challenging him.

'Why ask that now? Is it so important?' she countered.

'You can say that? Have you no shame? You mean you were not a virgin; you are not even apologetic. You let me sleep with you, yet you put on this innocent air, but I bet you are an expert, you are not even ashamed.' Ete Kamba had completely lost control of himself. He was now ranting, the image of a wounded innocent lover. He involuntarily began to shake Nko.

She followed his movements with cold eyes. Her mouth gathered as if she was about to spit, but she did not, only watched him. When the shake was becoming rather too painful, she said hoarsely: 'let me be. You are now in your university, you have achieved your, ambition, now it's time to fault your old friends. You don't have to do it this way. I am sure you'll find plenty of sophisticated virgins in this place of high learning. Let me be please!'

'Were you a virgin? Or are you still one? Swear that you are a virgin.' Ete Kamba continued as if he had not heard her.

A faint mocking derisive smile spread over her narrow unmade face. 'I swear to nothing. It is unchristian to swear.'

'Unchristian! Unchristian! Just hear her. Unchristian.' Ete Kamba mocked as he released her. 'What do you say to a girl who is not married and yet not a virgin? Is that Christian? What Christian girl would let herself be disvirgined by the wall? If you were a virgin, which I'm quite sure you were not - I went to check - you see, so I know. There was not a drop of blood. You are a prostitute, a whore, and you keep putting on this air of innocence as if you were something else. A whore, a shameless prostitute!' Ete Kamba was spluttering. Great anger twisted his young face. He felt really wronged.

Nko lifted her eyes and looked at him and then suddenly burst into tears. She made blindly for the door, but Ete Kamba would not let her go. 'You must tell me the truth. You are not leaving this place until I know the truth.'

'That is the truth.' Nko was raising her voice, and now protecting herself with her hands. 'Let me go. This place is full of girls, elegant girls. So let me go. If I am not a virgin, and I am a prostitute as you said, then let me go.' Her head shot up, her mouth puckered. Ete Kamba was beginning to associate this type of demeanour with her anger. And then she announced, 'look, we are friends, and can still go on being friends. I am not asking you your past, why don't you let mine be?'

'Oh, my God, to think my parents were even entertaining the hope of my marrying you?' Ete Kamba lamented.

Nko smiled. 'And now that you think I am not a virgin, they will not approve of me?'

'I wonder what they will think of a girl who allowed any man to sleep with her by the wall of a half-finished house.'

'You did not sleep with me, you stood with me. You pressed me to the wall. I had no choice. "You were that determined, that strong, that desperate. I simply did not stand a chance. You enjoyed it: I noticed that, and I had thought . . . Oh, my God, I was a fool.' She started to cry again. 'I had thought that, that was my way of showing you that I cared, that I was happy for your success. I ran the risk, knowing it could lead to pregnancy, but I wanted to make it a full and happy day for you. If that has cheapened me in your eyes, well I am sorry.' She wiped her eyes with the edge of her scarf, sniffing like a child, and again made for the door. At the door she turned and added, 'you called me a prostitute because of that, but you forgot that it takes two people at least to make any woman a prostitute, by your definition. You seem to be forgetting the men who slept with the woman. So if I am one, then what are you?'

'Men are never prostitutes. I have never heard of men being called prostitutes,' he cried.

'I have read of male prostitutes.' Nko remarked slowly.

Ete Kamba did not know what came over him. Maybe the fact that she had the courage to reply to him the way she did. A good, well brought up girl should be wary of saying the word, 'prostitute'. All this was just too much. He knew himself to be a clever person and for that he thought he deserved someone who was intelligent, and yet able to be ordinary. He did not like the blatant, the loud and the obvious. He lost his cool, and he reacted the way his father would have reacted, like an ordinary village man, who cared for his woman and had little patience in talking her out of her evil ways. He resorted to the method he knew was the quickest and the most effective - the brutal near animal method. He started to beat her. 'You can't talk to me like that, in my room. No woman has the right to talk to me like that. . . my mother wanted me to marry you . . . you can't talk to me like that.'

'To hell with your mother!' Nko found herself saying as she struggled with him and freed herself. 'Stop quoting her. It's you who can't cope with reality.' Her voice had risen even higher.

There were repeated knocks on the door.

'That's it, your first day on campus.' Nko observed breathlessly as she turned her face away. She could not control her bitter tears now. She was so full of humiliation and self-pity. She had been wrong in letting Ete Kamba see her soft underbelly. Now he was driving spears into it. She wished she had kept her aloofness and had allowed him to go on guessing. But with his admission to the State University of Calabar, she had thought he would be sophisticated enough to understand how she felt towards him that night. Nko now realized that she had been wrong in her estimation, and that from the mistake of that night, Ete Kamba would never trust her. But despite all this, she still wanted him. She would like them to make it up and start all over again.

She did not lift her head to find out who it was that was at the door. She heard however, Ete Kamba apologizing for causing so much noise, and promising that it would not happen again. 'Yes,' he was saying, 'all is well now.' He said he was only having an argument with his girlfriend. And he added conspiratorially in a stage whisper, 'You know what they are when they get themselves elated unnecessarily.' A low snigger had greeted this statement and the student left.

Minutes later, they lay both physically and mentally exhausted on his narrow student's bed. Nko had a kind of hollow emptiness inside her. Her face was expressionless. She felt neutralized. She had allowed Ete Kamba to take her again because she said to herself, 'what is there to lose now?'

She needed to pull herself together, but she needed time. And whilst she was waiting for the time, it did not matter to her one way or the other what Ete Kamba had done with her body. She had started by being passive and still, whilst he had brutally and desperately penetrated deeper and deeper inside her, so deep that she could feel him thrusting at the mouth of her womb. He was desperate, he was searching for the virginal blood his mother and friends had talked to him so much about. He was not quite sure he went all the way the first time. This time he was going to make sure he did it right. He dug, he groped, then he despaired. His mind was wandering. He felt so small, just like that little boy who had been holding his mother's lappa in a big market, and by some mishap let go of the lappa. His mother had gone far deeper into the market, searching for him and he was here searching for his mother. He was now wandering looking for her. He was now in tears, very alone, very lost.

He had previously imagined himself the first of all men, taking possession, hurting, conquering his bleeding partner whose blood would have washed them both almost like a living sacrifice. He would have happily hurt her, going through that masculine profound anguish. She would have started by whimpering until she would involuntarily burst out, letting out a yell of pain, whilst her pair of young black limbs opened and closed in painful joy; her hands, clawing the air, and her young body heaving and gyrating in bitter sweet innocent pain - a pain that would un-innocent her. He would have liked to be that prehistoric man, that ancient lamp bearer lighting her way from innocence into maturity. And he would have liked to hold her there, forever and forever. He would have liked her to die before him, so no one, no other man would share her. Oh, how he would have loved her, how he would have held her, cherished her, this innocent, yet educated, not so young modern African woman of his dreams.

But this... this... oh God, not this. His mouth was dry.

He sighed deeply and lifted his head to look at Nko afresh. He wondered what she was thinking. That maybe he was not good enough. How many men had she had before, he wondered torturing his troubled mind the more. He balanced his head on his hand and asked seriously. 'Can you promise me one thing, Nko?'

'What is it?' Her voice was remote, flat and without expression. She was weary. A voice that said, "I have had enough".

'That you will never sleep with any man but me.'

For once the thought crossed her mind that after all was? said and done, this handsome young man, who had everything a man could want, this man of her dreams, was really torturing himself. He was actually in trouble, and he was suffering. That he was not being wicked, that he was looking for a woman he would like to own and possess. Pity mingled with fear swept over her. What a tremendous responsibility! For her to go on being able to look after this man, to go on assuring him even though outwardly he showed false feelings of self-confidence. She forgot her hurt, and the pains he had inflicted on her. She felt sorry for him. Then she attempted to lighten his mood, giggled and said, 'or even stand with one. We stood by the wall remember? Would you have minded so much if the house had been finished with a roof, would it have been less painful?'

'Why do you want me to hate you, Nko?'

She breathed deeply before she answered slowly. 'On the contrary, I love you. I want you to love me too. But you don't seem to know what you want. I want you as you are, as against your wanting me as you think I ought to be. And that's the difficulty, presently a slight one, which can become unnecessarily important, or can even be forgotten. The choice is yours.'

'You have to wash that face,' he said unconnectedly.

'Don't worry, my parents won't know.'

Ete Kamba shook his head. He watched her get into a straight skirt, with a slit on the side, a shirt-like pale pink blouse and her black sandals. He noticed then that her dress was becoming smarter, she had changed from the school-girlish things she used to wear. He remarked, 'I like your skirt.'

'Yes, I do too. Mother made it for me. She thinks I should smarten myself up now that my fiancé is in a university. She thinks we'll get married when we are both through with our exams and things.'

'Would you like that yourself?'

She turned, looked at him and replied, 'yes,' rather faintly, as her eyes seemed not to be seeing him but something else beyond, like somebody looking into space and into the unknown future.

'I would like that too, but I wish you were more like my mother.'

Nko's eyes came down all of a sudden and she asked, 'how do you mean?'

'Mother is easy to understand. No little secrets with her.'

'Really?' Nko asked, the half mockery coming back into her voice again. 'You were so surprised at the party you had the night you got your results, were you not?'

'Yes.'

'Did your mother tell you that she was so worried about you that she had to go to Calabar for your results on Tuesday and was not going to spring the party on you until you went yourself. How else did you think I could have made that journey within an hour of your getting your results?'

'My mother!' Ete Kamba cried.

'Yes, your mother. A woman who tells all is no longer a woman. Our little secrets make us women; they are part of our survival kit. For what it's worth, I am a one man girl, and you are good enough for me.'

'For how long? You don't seem to care whether you marry or not.'

'That's not fair. I want marriage, but if none is available, you want me to commit suicide?'

'A woman who is not married is better off dead.' Ete Kamba declared uncompromisingly.

'You are so ancient, but refreshing.'

He walked her down to the taxi place, her eyes were still down, her face still swollen. But now he knew that she knew many, many things. Could he cope with a woman like that?

'Isa, for the love of God, please turn that thing down. We all know you are Hausa, you don't have to force that fact down our throats.'

'My tribe has nothing to do with it, Ete Kamba. I am a theatre artist, remember? So I'm afraid you have to get used to my native cultural background - I need it to write a new Hausa based play.'

'Hmmm, write a play in this hell of a place? Don't you have to think at all when writing? I don't know how you can do it! It beats me.' Ete Kamba cried.

'Not all of us love silences, the way you do, Ete Kamba. You are sometimes so still, Buddha-like, thinking. What great thoughts are going in that head of yours anyway? Sometimes I am curious. Man, this is your first year at a university, you should be happy, you can never be this age again.'

'Oh shut up and mind your bloody business. When did you become a preacher? Flippant like a woman - you are that most of the time. Noisy too.'

There were heavy knockings on the door. They sounded as if the person was hitting the door with head, hands and feet at the same time. Ete Kamba lifted his eyes in mock resignation. Isa was near hysterical, laughing - then said jokingly, 'look, Ete Kamba, let us hide under our beds so that we can say we do not want visitors, because you are in the English Department and are so deeply engrossed in thought, and because you are going to be the greatest poet Africa has ever seen. How is that?' He finished in counterfeit seriousness.

'Go to hell and stay there,' Ete Kamba spat.

Akpan burst into the room. His moon face was shining and his little mouth spread out into a smile. You were so busy arguing with each other that you did not hear me knock, so I had to come in uninvited.'

'Don't go into elaborate excuses, Akpan. You've gained access, you are now here, so welcome. What will you like to drink Scotch or Gin and Tonic?'

The boys laughed. 'Ete Kamba, you are reading too many? novels. You are one of those who think that after leaving here; you will get an elegant wife, live in a three room bungalow; with a Nigerian Assembled Peugeot car in the drive. No chance, my friend. You'll be lucky to be a head teacher in a village school, with a dusty, badly built house and a motorcycle . . . Scotch indeed. Come down to earth my friend' Akpan said.

He noticed that the others did not laugh this time. The idea of university education a decade ago had been all that Akpan had just said. But now high living costs were fast eroding the salaries of the academics, one had to go all the way for a Ph.D., to be able to live the way Akpan had just described. And an intelligent working wife was a must. Akpan was taken aback. He was ill at ease in that his friends should have taken what he had blurted out on the spur of the moment so seriously. For him these were the facts of lift which he did not allow himself to be bothered by. He would get by, he had always told himself. People who were less educationally equipped got by, why not him? There was one thing he was good at, that was changing the conversation especially from a morbid one like this to something lighter, So he asked, 'what were you two arguing about anyway?'

'We were not arguing, we were, believe it or not, talking. It's your townsman, you see, he does not want to be disturbed.' Isa, Ete Kamba's roommate explained in his beautifully modulated voice which is one of the adoring heritages bequeathed by God to most of those people whose mother tongue is Hausa. This voice, this languid gesture, is denied those Nigerians from the South. Some can never speak any foreign tongue intelligently without adulterating it with their native intonation. Just like an educated Indian who had never gone beyond Calcutta or Delhi. But the Hausas somehow did not have that problem. The same happens to them when they speak other European languages like French or German. Because of this and because of their unusually tall bodies, narrow near-Arabic features of the desert people, and the fact that they rightly insist on their elegant flowing robes, they are very popular in Theatre Arts. When the native Nigerian cultural arts comes, into its own, the Northerners will be very, very prominent. Already one can begin to see the great diplomatic roles they are playing among Nigerians' friends abroad. The Theatre Arts department is a good training ground for those going into politics and the diplomatic service. The Northerners are not doing too badly for Nigeria and for Africa in these fields. Meanwhile their students, like Isa and many others, are learning the theories from Caribbean and European artists who have come to work in Nigeria on a contract basis.

Akpan now looked at Ete Kamba and said rather insensitively, 'He had always been a dark horse - I suppose that makes him the more physically appetizing to the opposite sex. I was in the same school house with him.'

'Oh for God's sake, Akpan, stop talking about me as if I am not here.' Ete Kamba started to protest.

But Isa quickly jumped on to the bandwagon, 'you mean he is putting it on just to be what, did you say - "physically appetizing". Oh, you people from the English Department - you do make up nice phrases, "physically appetizing".' He chewed the last phrase thoughtfully, rubbing the sparse beard he had been trying to sprout for months. He strode from one end of the room to another, muttering, 'physically appetizing.'

Ete Kamba and Akpan laughed. They could see that Isa was performing. So difficult for some of those who worked in the Theatre Arts to divorce acting from reality. One could always tell them apart on campus - they dressed louder than anyone else, they looked fitter because of all those gyrating movements the Caribbean artist was making them do. The others noticed too that Isa was walking on his toes, something that had now become almost second nature to him.

'I am sure that phrase is going to be in his new play. You know he is writing a play, don't you?' Ete Kamba addressed Akpan wickedly.

'Oh, are you going to write about sword fighting and horsemen?' Akpan asked cynically.

Isa stopped in his tracks and with his head thrown dramatically to one side and one finger over his mouth, said, 'maybe, maybe. You won't deny the fact that those men on horses are physically appetizing, especially when compared to the poor specimens from this area, what do they call you again, the Ibibios. Is it true that Ibibio means small. Why are most of your men only five feet tall...'

Akpan descended on him, shouting, 'shut up, shut up, you Moslem, shut up.'

Ete Kamba made sure he removed his portable radio, so that the two wrestling students would not break it. Then he called, 'for God's sake, Akpan, did you come here to fight? You were knocking, no, kicking is the right word, as if you wanted to borrow something...'

They stopped and Akpan was breathing heavily, his paunchy stomach going up and down. Sweat was already all over his face. 'No,' he breathed, 'actually I brought peace, I mean good news.'

'Oh, that is nice, for somebody who brought good news, you have not done too badly at all. Look at the state of our room. Ete Kamba and I spent hours this morning putting everything in order. See what you have done to it.'

'Violence and religious good news go hand in hand. Jesus brought the good news, but how many millions of people have been slaughtered in the name of the good news. You remember what they reported that an Indian chief said in New Mexico when the Catholic Spaniards had killed all his tribe in order to force him to become a Christian? He said "If these type of people are going to inhabit the so called Heavens, I'll rather go to hell and stay with my ancestors." He refused to accept the good News.'

'What happened to him then?' Isa asked, rather curious.

'Because they could not win him for Christ,

they burnt him alive, and the rest of his people and took his land from him and planted the Spanish flag. That is how they won that part of South America for Christ.'

'I hate such stories. Makes you wonder, whether our people here dancing *Alleluya* praise the Lord everyday are doing the right thing,' Ete Kamba mused.

'Well it's not doing them any harm, is it? Can you imagine this place without religion? The fear of hellfire - people really believe in it you know - the fear of that fire makes the steward put in at least a few token days' work for his master,' Akpan said.

'Oh, don't be so cynical, Akpan.' Isa snapped. 'You mean our people did not have any sense of decency before the arrival of this "*Alleluya* praise the Lord thing?"'

'I am not going to argue with you. What I come to tell you is that there is that Revival this evening. You must have seen their leaflets, I'm sure Ete Kamba knew all about it.'

'Yes indeed, is it today? Honestly, I have quite forgotten all about it. Are you actually going, after all you have been saying?

'Ah, as students, we are to keep an open mind on such things. We must not be frightened to expose ourselves to new ideas, because otherwise, we will not be able to make rational conclusions.'

'Oh Allah, on whose side is he now? Have you got a girlfriend there at the Religious Revival. One minute you condemn them, the next you want us to go and listen to their wailings and breast beatings.'

'Yes, I have a girlfriend there.' Akpan declared flatly, looking serious.

'Do we know her, have we ever had the pleasure?'
Ete Kamba asked.

'Yes you have met her many, many times. In fact
you go to her every day.'

'Oh? Who is she?'

'I'll tell you Ete Kamba since you are my best
friend. Come here bring your ear...'

Isa burst out laughing. 'I hate secrecies. It shows a
sign of weakness. The woman must be the ugliest
person on campus or old enough to be your great
grandmother or something.'

Akpan ignored Isa and whispered something to
Ete Kamba. The latter started laughing. 'So that is it.
You have no chance, not even in hell. She is old
enough to be your mother and moreover, she is
married. You are pulling our legs of course. Can you
imagine Akpan and Dr Mrs Edet in bed, Isa? Can
you, even in dreams conjure such a picture?'

All of them laughed until tears came into
Akpan's eyes.

'And seriously, do we have to go?' Ete Kamba
asked, looking suddenly worried. He so wished to be
alone, free from these diversions.

'Well if as their leaflets say - God is coming down
today and has chosen our Unical as His landing
canvas, I wouldn't like to miss it. Most of the students
are going through. Let us go. I hate to disappoint that
lady. She has a look about her, so remote, and with
that ostrich-like neck, to say nothing of those camel-
like legs ... no I won't like to disappoint her,' Akpan
said dreamily.

'Oh watch it, Mister, she is married you know. But
wait a minute, is her husband not among the

members of her church?' Ete Kamba asked.

'I don't know really. All I know is that that professor from Nbamkpa is more or less the leader of the group, well on this campus anyway. I have heard so much about this Professor Ikot. He is such an enigma, able to combine academic work with the spiritual one. They say he sees visions and speaks in tongues and that his rhetoric prayers can really move the earth. Dr Mrs Edet, is his helper, I think.' Akpan expanded.

'His rhetoric prayers can really move the earth - oh, Akpan how you exaggerate! And, Akpan, that is a diabolical claim. How can you say a thing like that of a man who works so closely with another's wife? Is that the reason why she always insists on being addressed as Sister, Dr Mrs Ngana Edet? She needs all those titles to achieve a fulfilment in her personality, and maybe to assure her husband that there is nothing funny going on between her and our illustrious professor!'

'Eh, I don't say I believe in Professor Ikot's sanctimonious rhetoric. I am just curious, that's all. And you know what a relative of mine who had stayed two decades abroad said. That this love of many titles is a Nigerian thing. You know there are comparatively few Nigerian females who have achieved the position of being a Doctor in their education. So, the American trained ones in particular, would like people to know that they are doctors, and despite that, they are still presentable and beautiful enough to hook an unfortunate man. So you see how these new females overburden themselves.' Akpan said so imperiously, that for a while no one could dispute or add to his claim.

Then Ete Kamba felt obliged to continue. 'These women! You know what I think about them, I think they want to eat their cakes and to have them at the same time,' Ete Kamba observed.

'I think though that those women from the highly industrialized countries do know what they are talking about. Many of their academics, married or not, may or may not use all their tides. Look at that German scientist, she calls herself simply Ulla, and on her door, puts Ulla Saber. It was later that I knew that she was not only a doctor but a professor in her country before coming here. And some of those highly qualified surgeons in the Medical school call themselves just "Mr!"' Akpan said rather seriously.

'Well as they say in a country of the blind ... I am quite sure our surgeons would call themselves, Dr, Mr Chief so and so.' Ete Kamba reasoned.

The young men laughed rather easily.

'It's pathetic though, you read about immortal writers like Maugham and others refusing doctorate titles, even though they had moderated many of the doctorate theses written about them. But did you read about that Nigerian novelist who claimed that because he had written so many pamphlets and because some Nigerians have become professors just by studying him, he should be given a doctorate?' Ete Kamba asked.

'I think the man - you mean Ebenezer Angus - well he has a point. And I don't agree with you. Many of his books are pamphlets of eighty or ninety pages or so, but he has written three or four of what I would regard as classics.' Isa defended.

'Ah, that is because you are in Theatre Arts and are used to reading few page plays. When you have conditioned yourself to reading works like those of Leon Uris, Frederick Forsyth and even Alex Hailey's *Roots,* you will understand what I mean.'

'Ete Kamba, you mean you really read those heavies?' Akpan asked, his brow raised.

Isa started to laugh. 'I thought you said you were in the same dormitory together. You wait, just come and see.' He went to Ete Kamba's corner and brought out *Trinity,* by Leon Uris, *Exodus,* and *Mila Eighteen* all by the same author, and said, 'none of these is less than five hundred pages. One book from this author is tantamount to twenty by our Ebenezer Angus. So you see he had gone beyond that. He does not need that kind of title.'

'Whew! just think of being able to write books like that. If I can only write one, that big, I wouldn't mind if I never wrote again.' Ete Kamba said whimsically.

'You can if you try. But most Nigerian writings are not creative. They are usually political or a collection of speeches by this or that person. We have not got the really big creators like Uris and the other. But Ngugi with his *Petals of Blood* is almost there judging by the size of it. I have not read it, but it's probably political otherwise he would not have been treated the way he was treated by his government.' Ete Kamba said.

'In that case, I'm hopeful. We will soon get there, and knowing Africans, judging from the way we have forged ourselves in music and sports, we will soon surpass them. Is Ngugi a Doctor?'

'I don't think so, and I hope not. He is one of our

greatest writers if not *the* greatest. He has left university life now, so he would be able to write more and in depth,' Ete Kamba replied.

'Well I must go now. I will look forward to seeing you at the Revival. Ete, can I borrow your *Trinity* for a week?'

Ete Kamba laughed, really amused. 'I would like you to have it, but I know you Gabriel Akpan, you will not get beyond twenty pages at most. You haven't got the patience.'

'What he is trying to tell you is that you are not a cultured African. You still long for short moonlight stories.' Isa explained.

'Oh go to hell both of you. I think you deserve each other.' Akpan said and stormed out.

Uneasy silence fell in the room. Both boys knew that they would have to go to that Revival. Ete Kamba's interest had been roused in Professor Ikot, who came from the same village as Nko. Maybe he would be able to help him find himself.

8. Spiritual Diet

It had rained in the late afternoon, very much towards the evening and the spaces of Malabor were refreshingly fresh and mushy. It was now early night, and the thick tropical night had suddenly taken over from the bright wet clammy day. There were no electric lights in Malabor, but the ones in the dining-hall and those escaping from the many windows of the hostel situated in the surrounds, illuminated the area not a bit. Students, male and female, in their different colourful clothes, moved leisurely in and out of the shadows into the pockets of light. There was that moist wet feeling in the air. Everything and everybody was so limp, lethargic, leisurely and slow.

The scene in Malabor this evening had been made richer by the presence of many cars. There were many lecturers with families and friends, and many strange women in identical clothes - dresses with long balloon sleeves, and matching pieces tied round their heads. The dresses went from their necks to their ankles. Some women members of the Revivalist Group, no doubt. The cars were now so numerous, that they spilt onto the pathway; the lecturers' Volkswagen beetles were parked cheek by jowl with those belonging to the showier class: the ever-present Peugeot cars - mainly cream or off white in colour. This night their creaminess helped in relieving the dark and otherwise dreary atmosphere.

Ete Kamba, wearing some lightweight trousers he had bought in Aba, and a Marks and Spencer's wine coloured shirt one of the lecturers' wives had sold him, sauntered with his roommate, Isa, towards the dining-hall. They were both tall young men, very much aware of their handsomeness. Ete Kamba always tried to play his down by being cool and detached when in company, but Isa never bothered to do that. His discipline made him rather undisciplined. They knew they had to pass by the girls' hall of residence, the famous Hall Two. They knew that on a night like this, when there was a do on campus and in the dining-hall, the most of them would be looking out to follow the proceedings that were going on around them. The girls did look out and giggled and made quiet comments, but the young men pretended not to notice.

Moonface Akpan had gone before them to make sure he had his supper hot. He hated cold food even in clammy weather like this one. And he had suspected, and rightly too, that on a night like this, when there was going to be a big do in the dining-hall, students would have to be hurried. Akpan, already sporting a slightly pouchy belly, not only liked his foot hot, but like to take his time to chew, meditate while chewing and enjoy every bit of it. So he had to go in before the others. They, in their own turn, did not bother to look for him: they knew he would be there already.

When inside the hall, Ete Kamba and Isa and many others had to be shooed to the back of the hall for their trays of food. The front of the hall had already been taken – soft, cozy chairs were arranged in front, next to the stage, and many helpers, especially the women, in their funny, long all enveloping dresses were busy arranging them in rows. There were so many people and even children were enjoying the confusion - running here and there and in between adults enjoying the little freedom they knew would soon be followed by a long disciplined evening. There was no doubt about it, the Reverend Professor Ikot and his helper Sister Dr Mrs Edet, had really done their homework.

When his friends had left him alone earlier on, Ete Kamba looked around for the innumerable tracts he had been given telling him all about this meeting. From them he found out that this spiritual group originated from America. They claimed to have performed many miracles through prayers and also had given peace of mind to many students. He had been looking forward to his university life, but since moving into campus, he could not push Nko out of his mind. He tried very hard to do this, but could not. His friends did not guess that beneath his wide easy grin and confident air, his mind was troubled. He had so far covered all this with his natural charm and cultivated personal gloss.

During his school days, he could talk about it to his father. But after the gruntings he heard his father make and to make matters worse, his mother's sickly voice, he knew then, that somehow he had been weaned. He hated and loved Nko. He hated her so much that many a time she had made him angry, he had planned all the things he would do and say when next he met her. But when she appeared, her little cute face that somehow did not lose the pert childishness in it, and her naive way of tightly tying her scarf covering her highbrow as if she were a nun, aroused the protectiveness in him. He would become so protective that many a time he had to hold himself tight when he saw her being extra nice conversationally with his friends Isa and Akpan. He did not want to discuss her with them. And sometimes he noticed that there was a kind of envy mingled with respect amongst them in that he never really looked about the campus for another girl, even though there were so many classically beautiful girls with money who normally frequented such institutions of higher learning.

So he was very keen on coming to the Revival, because after it, he was going to discuss his problem with the Reverend Professor Elder Ikot. The Reverend had been in this university for all the six years since its inception, so he would have dealt with cases like his. All he wanted was a neutral person to talk to. For that, it was worth leaving one's comparatively peaceful hostel room and coming to this crowded place on an evening like this.

And if he should lose his nerve and decide not to talk to him, he would talk to the white Americans who he knew would come to this Revival. After all, it had all started in America. And three quarters of the staff on campus were trained in America, so the university was run along American liberal lines rather than on the British elitist ones. Being a young university, statistics had not yet been compiled to show how well the students from this State University were doing in civilian walks of life after leaving campus. But Ete Kamba was sure they had done well, and that the academic standard was quite high.

Even though the undergraduates had been told that the dining-hall would be needed tonight and that they should come and have their supper early, many were determined to take their time. They kept coming in and going out, banging their spoons on their plates and scratching their chairs on the cement floor, causing a lot of commotion as if determined to disrupt the meeting.

Professor Ikot and Sister Dr Mrs Edet stood by the large door leading off the stage and watched all these goings on. They consulted their watches several times and Sister Dr Mrs Edet who always prided herself as the child of God, and never the pushful type, said in her masculine voice, 'I hope they are not in their anti-everything mood tonight.'

Professor Elder Ikot laughed uneasily. He knew that one could never tell with students. Any minor thing could precipitate a demonstration and interruption. He did not want anything of that kind to happen tonight. He had prepared himself, mentally and physically for this meeting. So he said, 'I hope not! I'll give them exactly five minutes and then we'll start. If we start by singing any of our popular choruses, it will drown their orchestrated noises and delays.' Sister Dr Mrs Edet giggled like a silly schoolgirl, her hand covering her mouth, a childish gesture which was wasted on her rather tall man-like figure. Her tall, skinny, near flat chested figure looped in the dark shadow by the dining-hall door like a giraffe hunting for fruits from the top of a tree. One minute her head, which she had now covered in a red velvety affair looped in, and the next one it looped out, saying intermittently, 'these students, they are still there.' This woman was tall, she was skinny and she was dark. She was very religious - the

American gospel type which was gaining ground fast in this part of the world. The pan of the world that was still called the Third World by the so-called industrial countries. They were wrong in many aspects like education, and the rich living of the very rich. But when it came to religion, Africa was just finding her own stand. Her people were still in the early hysterical stages of the ancient apostles who would do nothing but keep praising God with the hope that Jesus Christ would come and liberate them within forty days or so. When they received the Holy Ghost some of them were beginning to realize that when Jesus said that 'it was not for you to know the time or the season,' He was right. Equally, 'His second coming' may be symbolic like most of His philosophical sayings. For many people in Nigeria and for many black Americans and West Indians, whose education was very low or non-existent, and who because of life's demands have really not been able to recapture the art of deep thinking, which was once mastered by their ancestors - going about the streets shouting '*Alleluya* Jesus is coming now' was easier to understand. It gave them a sense of importance as well. Like Dr Mrs Sister Edet. When she told her colleagues that she was the child of God, she would look at you with her long neck craned, as if she expected you to fall over yourself in admiration, or in envy or even in gratitude, that she had been able to talk to you. It gave her a sense of power, not very much over her colleagues, who laughed uneasily and accepted her simply because she was there to be accepted; but the power she and Professor Ikot held over the students and the low workers in the town was disgusting to behold. Almost like that Reverend John Jones in Georgetown, who had controlled the thinking of over nine hundred people, causing them to commit that horrible mass suicide. One would have thought that incidents like that and many exposures of so many Jesuses in the capital, Lagos, would have hardened people. But they did not. People did not want to think. These Elders and prophets did the thinking for them, they encouraged them to dance, jump and roll on the floor, beat their chests, work out their frustrations on themselves, then go home tired and empty, to build up energy on their scanty diets, for the next breast beating session. Of course all these things were not free. They always had to dip into their pockets to contribute to this cause or to that one. A pathetic situation, but good in that it kept people who had not been trained to be responsible for their actions, quiet. If they knocked their foot against a stone because they were not looking, that was God's will. A little girl lost her life on her way back from school because it was raining and the open gutters carried her away. Her father, instead of urging the government to cover these open unhealthy gutters on both sides of the road, said it was God's will. The gutters were still there, still slimy, still green, bringing up foul smells, to make any stomach turn. They were also a big danger for most pedestrians who had in mind the mad traffic and the crazy motorcyclists. Of course, those in the big decision making positions didn't walk. Like Professor Ikot and Sister Dr Mrs Edet, they glided around in their chauffeur driven cars. And in most cases, to make sure that the drivers did their work with the slave like devotion they required, they would employ only those from their gospel church.

The five minutes soon expired, and the Reverend Professor urged the brass band group specially invited for this night onto stage where they started playing the tune of a popular chorus which Sydney Pokier made even more popular in his film with the nuns called, 'Amen.' So 'Amen', and 'Amen' started sounding from one end of the mighty hall to the other. The religious brothers and sisters who were outside, waiting for the students to finish their meal, jumped into Christian consciousness. They all boomed with the hefty brass band players and started the chorus, 'Amen ... A... men. A... men. A... men. Amen.'

Soon the hall was full, everybody joined in, the music got heated, the Professor took the microphone and would say, 'Jesus in the desert.' And the crowd would answer, 'Amen.' This was repeated so many times. Children who were running around before, simply being children, were now clapping and swaying their heads from side to side. And as for those women in the long dresses, they had taken up a corner of the stage - they must be members of the choir or something.

Most people, especially the Africans, love music. And community singing of any sort, be it the village ballad or the pop one or whatever never ceases to appeal. Few popular musicians from abroad would make any mark if they played and expected Nigerians to sit for hours simply listening and giving out applause at the right times. If they had to repeat their performance, they would find the hall almost empty. Here people had to take part, either by dancing their part or responding as they were now doing with the 'A...mens.' So students who had originally come to cause a disturbance and delay their eating time longer than they normally did, put down their trays of food, and joined in the community chorus singing. After only a few minutes of this musical arousal, some began to use their trays and spoons to add to the melodious din. Soon the Reverend Professor, raised his hands in an effort to make a Jesus-like gesture, but he failed, just like his female helper who was desperately trying to be feminine, but whose height and flat chestedness had robbed her of any real feminine attributes.

The Professor was stocky, compactly built. He dressed expensively, always in a three piece suit, which always looked too tight in a place as hot as this. He gave out an air of stuffiness, overweight, and the appearance of somebody who tries too hard. Whereas his assistant, Sister Dr Mrs Edet was tall, he was short. And because of his over dressing, he looked shorter still. He now spread his short arms wide, sweat pouring down his face and started another popular chorus called, 'He has the whole world in His hand.' Of course the crowd took it up, and people were dancing openly, laughing and clapping.

Ete Kamba and Isa could no longer eat in peace. They handed over their trays and were lucky to find a place to sit at the back of the hall. The cooks had now cleared everything away, and the religious people had completely taken over. Even the cooks and all the dining-hall workers were by now singing and swaying. 'If you can't beat them, you have to join them' Isa shouted to his friend.

Ete Kamba nodded, and then mouthed, 'but you are a Moslem!'

What?' shouted Akpan, who had by now joined them.

'I said Isa is a Moslem.'

'Have you seen a very religious Moslem at prayers? He goes like this, up and down, and then his head on the ground like this.' Akpan was not just saying all this he was illustrating his words with actions. Of course the Christian faithfuls next to him did not think it odd, they too were busy with acrobatic movements of their own. Isa and Ete Kamba almost burst their lungs in their vain efforts to control their laughter. Looking at Akpan and at the Reverend Professor pounding on the microphone and the Child of God, Sister Dr Mrs Edet, flapping and looping her body this way and that, the first reaction was to laugh. But they soon stopped laughing, when Akpan ended his funny movements and the movements of those on the stage had lost their novelty. By the time they ended the chorus, the spirit of the Revival was on everybody. The Reverend Professor, raised his stumpy arms once more, and shouted, '*Alleluya*' and the congregations resounded with a deafening '*Alleluya*!'

He repeated this so many times, that again people started to raise their arms up and to spin around, screaming, '*Alleluya*!'

Then he led the now worked up mob into prayer. That prayer was another art in self arousal. The prayer was long, it was lusty, it was soaring. All delivered in bellowing rhetoric. Each forceful sentence was followed by resounding 'Amens' and '*Alleluya*s'. He worked himself up, swinging the microphone in the air, bellowing into it, then collecting his dumpy body and jumping up and down in religious ecstasy, the jacket of his three piece suit flapping up and down like angry elephant ears. When he eventually lowered his voice, simply because he was tired and was becoming dangerously out of breath, he started in a lower key to utter some gibberish in a funny strange tongue, and the music man started to drone his drum as if to punctuate all the rubbish the Reverend Professor was saying, the effect of that was to make the congregation more excited. Then he stopped dramatically and shouted, 'God is here, come forward and confess your sins, come and ask for forgiveness.'

The stampede that followed was indescribable. Then Ete Kamba could see why those people in Georgetown could have killed themselves. If this Reverend Professor had asked them all to go and kill themselves, because God was there, they would have gladly done so, singing '*Alleluya*' all the way, and woe betide anyone who tried to stop them.

The pushing and jostling were so much that Ete Kamba had to open his eyes in order to see and be able to protect himself if need be. The front part of the stage was now filled with crying people, some banging their heads on the wall. A woman was busy tearing her well-made hair apart. Everybody was screaming and crying. Ete Kamba was surprised to see that his arms were raised, in an appealing way. He was able to control himself a little, to look at some of the junior lecturers. And, as for the students, they were doing most of the crying. The music man was droning the drum, one beat at long intervals, and the

Reverend Professor was saying in a low menacing voice, *'yeah,* confess; yeah, confess.'

Ete Kamba looked for his friends, but they were no longer standing by him. He looked widely around and was shocked to see Isa, jumping up and down and saying things like, 'Allah, please forgive.' It was then Ete Kamba knew that this was no laughing matter, that this Professor must really be a great person. He would go to him. If he had this power over hundreds of people and was able to rouse and control them in this way, there must be something about him. He may not believe in being hysterical in his own way of praying, but he would look this man up.

They sang many, many songs and choruses after this, Isa got sober, and there were bumps ballooning on Akpan's face, nonetheless by the time they made their way back to their rooms, they all felt empty and also fulfilled somehow.

'I am hungry,' Akpan moaned. But he was ignored. His friends' thoughts were far away.

9. The Trusted Elder

The Cultural Faculty building was one of those buildings on campus that Ete Kamba had never really visited. It was like one of those landmarks, whose existence one was well aware of, but one never actually came round to questioning their being by going inside and finding out what it was that really was happening there. Ete Kamba, sauntered every morning past this cream coloured long building with blue edgings along its wide lattice windows, and never once ventured inside until now. He had to go in, for how else could he bare his troublesome heart to the Reverend Professor Ikot. Had not the Professor said the other night that any student who was worried should come to him so that he may help to lighten their burden? Ete Kamba knew that the Professor Elder Ikot had sounded like somebody reciting the Sermon on the Mount, but who else was there for the students to unburden their souls to?

Elder Professor Reverend Ikot's office was on the second floor. The steps leading to it were uttered with parts of broken desks and chairs. Students had left these piece hidden away so they could come for them when needed. There were never enough desks and chairs for many of the lectures, so these broken pieces were many a time invaluable. Ete Kamba would help himself to one of the tops of a desk that looked as if it was still in a good condition. He would do that on his way back from the Elder's office. When there, he knocked and was told to wait outside because there were so many students and lecturers wanting to have

a word with this unique spiritual leader. Ete Kamba
waited patiently.

It was true that he had to book this appointment
to see the Elder. It was equally true that the Elder
had specifically told him to come at eleven o'clock
in the morning, yet he could understand why the
Elder could not see him even though he made sure
to be there by eleven thirty, giving the elder a thirty
minutes 'African time' gap. Ete Kamba knew the
ways of these big men. If they asked you to come at
eleven and they saw you on that dot of eleven, that
might cheapen them in your eyes. So it was always
better, always safer for someone in the big posts to
appear almost inaccessible. Not only was it difficult
to get to the top, but when one was at the top, one
must mind one's ways not to cheapen oneself
before those still at the lower rungs. Ete Kamba had
thought that because he was approaching the Elder
on religious personal grounds, this Nigerian thing
of not allowing familiarity to breed contempt
would not apply. 'It's silly of me to expect to be
treated differently, just because he had said that in
the eyes of Jesus Christ, we are all equal. That does
not make us equal in the real sense.' With that
maxim as emotional survival armour, he was
willing to wait.

He was waiting in the middle of a long dark
corridor on to which offices of different lecturers
and professors opened. All of them had their names
and titles on the doors. One door facing him was
particularly interesting. Apparently the office was
shared by two women. The first woman was no
doubt one of those who put on themselves the

double yoke of modernity and that of tradition. She was a Chief, she was a Mrs, she was a Dr, her father's name seemed to be Iyang, and her married name was Bassey. She was determined to print all this information on her door, and to cap it all she was a Christian because the legend went on to challenge the reader by saying, 'Do you believe in miracles? I am one.' This woman was probably an ordinary lecturer because underneath all these was the name of another woman who was simply Mrs Prophetess Ekanem. The poor door looked like the page of a newspaper, so many letters, so much information. Ete Kamba remembered hearing Philip in his class say that he read an article somewhere, which said that non Nigerians marvel at this hunger of Nigerians for titles. There was a story of a top politician who cajoled and bribed and threatened the university in his state to give him a Doctorate degree. He was given one after a while, but the trouble now was that the man wanted to be made a professor. Academically, this politician stopped reading after he left his teacher training college over twenty years ago. 'I must ask Philip whether the man was eventually made a professor or not. Philip would know.'

Opposite to where he was standing were the corridor's loos. The stink was unbearable. It was so strong that he had to keep spitting when he knew that no one was watching. At one time it got so bad that he went towards the end of the corridor to talk to two young women who were busy plaiting their hair, and asked if they were the cleaners. One was polite enough to answer. The other ignored him and went on talking as if he never existed.

'That toilet, it's stinking the place out. Can't you do something about it?'

'Watin' you wan make we do, when we no geti water, whey we go use for flush, abi you wan make ago geti water from me mama well?'

Ete Kamba walked quietly away. One could never win with such women. If they were determined to get water with which to flush the basins every hour or so, they could have. But who was going to suggest that to them. They had finished the actual cleaning in the morning by about nine o'clock, so for the rest of the day, they just had to be seen around the building. They did not have to be actually doing anything, but had to be there all the same, for the Federal government was paying them full time till three thirty in the afternoon.

Ete Kamba consulted his watch for the umpteenth time. He was going to forgo all he had planned to do, just to see this man today. Eventually, at exactly two o'clock, he was asked to come in. The Professor and Elder was writing at his desk, and did not look up when he asked gutturally, 'yes?'

Ete Kamba introduced himself. He did not regard the elder's behaviour as rude. Maybe the Elder should have apologized for having kept him waiting for almost three hours, yet that would be like lowering one's dignity. Ete Kamba had been talking for about three minutes before Professor Ikot raised his head and looked at the young man for the first time.

'You said you are from these parts?' he asked in Efik.

'Yes, from Mankong, and the girl I have been talking about came from Nbamkpa.'

'I am from Nbamkpa too. So I should know her. Who is her father?'

'Udoh sir.'

'Udoh? You mean his little girl Nko? You mean Nko had allowed you to sleep with her; that innocent looking girl? Oh these girls, these girls . . .' Here he burst into rather fitful laughter. He reminded Ete Kamba of the figure he cut a few days ago on the stage when the 'Holy Spirit' was upon him and he was speaking with 'tongues'. His broad shoulders were shaking the same way, and his rather large head was lolling from side to side like that of a dragonfly about to die. But what cautioned Ete Kamba the more was the boorish language that emitted from his wide mouth. It was low: it was wild: it was animal-like. Ete Kamba did not know what he wanted the Elder's language to be like, but it was not anything like this. One thing he did know, this was not the sound he expected from the spiritual man of God. He would have turned round and walked out of the room, but he realized that he had inadvertently revealed a great deal about himself and about Nko. He was ambivalent towards Nko at that moment, but it was the type of ambivalence one sometimes had for one's loved ones - like a mother would sometimes tell a silly child, 'I hate you,' knowing full well that she did not mean it. And if the mother was lucky to find a fellow sufferer to talk things over with, somehow the feelings tended to blow over. All Ete Kamba wanted from this man concerning his first love was reassurance, not ridicule. He wanted strength from an older and experienced man. And from a man who had confessed publicly that he was a person of prayer.

Ete Kamba's eyes must have bored into the Elder's innermost soul for when he suddenly looked up, he seemed for the first time to be aware of the fact that there was someone else in the room. He stopped laughing, not immediately but gradually like a spoilt child who had been quietened with a sweet lolly. And just like that child, the Professor dribbled in his uncertain amusement.

He had the decency to wipe out his dribble with a surprisingly clean and expensive looking handkerchief. Ete Kamba had expected him to bring out a grubby ink stained affair which would have been in keeping with his gross, fat, short and uncultivated self.

'I know Nko,' he declared unnecessarily.

'Big deal.' Ete Kamba said to himself, but still stared at him.

'She is one of the most promising girls we have in my village. She is university material and nobody - nobody is going to prevent her from reading for a degree. She owes it to her parents and to us from our village. So my advice to you young man is to look for a girl that will suit you more. After all, you are here on a scholarship, you went to your Grammar school on a scholarship, you are more from the Ibibio tribe, your parents don't really belong to where you are now. Nko is from my part. She is a true Efik from Duke Town, and women from our part have always brought great honour to their families. She will be in this university in a year or two. So what do you want a graduate wife for? Why don't you get a trained teacher or a nurse or something? Let us pray, my boy, so that God will give you the wisdom to learn to sew your coat according to your measurements.'

Unthinking, Ete Kamba found himself kneeling down and praying for Nko's success, not because he wanted to but because he was shocked into passivity. They also prayed to God to send him his own rightful mate.

They soon ended the prayer, and the Reverend said now in his worldly-wise voice, that teachers who marry female graduates are looking for trouble. 'Take it from me,' he expanded, 'the best you can do after this place is to teach. A good headmaster at most. So, work hard at your studies and get a good degree.'

Here Ete Kamba recovered himself somewhat and asked shyly, 'and Nko, what type of man is she going to marry?'

'Oh, she is made for the Commissioner or the Professorial class, you know those on salary level sixteen and over. You'll be lucky to get level seven when you finish here.'

Ete Kamba smiled. Here it was permitted for the adult or the man at the top to be rude to the aspiring student, but a student who wanted to go back home with his certificate must learn to hold his tongue. Ete Kamba knew he had to do just that - hold his tongue. About his little problem with Nko, he left the Elder's office none the wiser.

10. *A Woman's Survival Armour*

Nothing could beat the excitement and hope with which girls like Nko looked at university life. It was one thing to go to secondary school and get good certificates, but to be really admitted into one of the highest institutions of the land, and with the hope of getting a degree at the end of it, was something else. She had regarded herself as an extremely lucky girl. She would make the best of it. She would work hard at her studies and she was going to get not just a degree, but a good one. Then she would marry Ete Kamba and they would have about six children. They were not going to lack anything because she would be working and Ete Kamba would be working as well. Theirs was going to be a good marriage, a marriage in which the two of them would complement each other.

One fly in the ointment was the new self she was beginning to acquire. Previously she would let Ete Kamba have his own way with where they went together and with whatever they were going to do. But now, she was beginning to ask questions, to ask him to give her his reasons for some of his actions. She hated herself after such questioning; she knew that Ete Kamba did not like it, and many a time she would promise herself never to do it again. 'For what is a woman if after all her degrees and what have you, she is not married?' She had asked herself often. Anyway, she had no problem on that score; her childhood sweetheart was still faithful to her. So she had to be very careful not to lose him.

She had confided in her mother about it. 'Mother, look at all the wahala he raised about the university forms the other day. He wanted to know how I managed to get the forms before any other person. I had to tell him that I needed the forms, and then that I got them, so what did it matter how? But he was still angry...'

Her mother smiled. She picked up Nko's young, smooth and still delicate hand in her rough hard one and said, 'and you told him that Professor Elder Ikot got them for you?'

'But mother, he got them for me. You remember mother, that father was very ill and I had to be with him in hospital, and for one reason or the other the forms were delayed, so he got them for me. Why should that annoy Ete Kamba, why, mother? I was speaking the truth, was I not, mother?'

'Nko, Nko, a few years ago, when Ete Kamba got his admission and you were not even sure you would be finishing secondary school to say nothing of going to a university, would you have told him the whole truth? Would you have had the courage to tell him that Professor Ikot got these forms for you? You knew he would be angry. If you didn't know that, then, my daughter, you were still not a woman. But I'm sure you know now.'

'Mother, Professor Ikot is a spiritual leader!'

'And he is a man.'

Nko remembered the incident on the night Ete Kamba loved her by the wall. She looked at her mother. Mother and child suddenly found themselves plunged into that kind of silence that is not loudly communicative. Unwittingly, Nko's arms circled

108

round her mother's neck and she cried with near anguish. 'Oh, mother, I want to have both worlds, I want to be an academician and I want to be a quiet nice and obedient wife, the type you all want me to be. I want the two, mother. Oh please, mother, help me. I know I can be of more use to you and my brothers if I had these two worlds.'

'I know, Nko, I know. You know sometimes I think you modern girls are not so lucky. When I was your age, all I was thinking of was how to go to the fattening room and make myself round and beautiful for your father. I did not have to sit up night after night with no sleep; I did not have to eat just oranges to keep myself thin; I did not even have to look for a husband. Now you have this new thing, this mad education for women and yet still, you want to have everything we had ... it is going to be difficult. We had to keep quiet, because we did not know many of the things our men knew. You may call us ignorant, but we were happy and contented in our ignorance.' Nko's mother sighed and then went on in a much more confident voice, 'I am sure Jesus Christ who said that all those who carry heavy yokes should come to Him, will help you. I think you should go to Him in prayer. Because, daughter, you know what you are under, you are under a double yoke. So you need a stronger shoulder with which to carry it. I did not carry this, so how can I help, enh? I, who like you is bewildered by it all.'

Nko had stood up and made as if to go to the door, then asked, 'Mother, suppose I refuse to take the university place given me now, do you think that that will make me happier?'

'I don't know, daughter. You have been to see your man friend at that place. You have seen that people who went to such places came out better equipped financially to cope with this expensive country. You have also seen that without money no one is respected here anymore. And you know that you can get all these things by going there. You have heard me shout with sheer joy on your admission to Unical, and you have seen my friends congratulate me on the one hand, and then envy me on the other hand, all for having such a brilliant daughter. Will you ever forgive yourself if you do not take the chance? And suppose at the end of it all, Ete Kamba became a really big man, who wanted an educated wife to match, where do you think you will be then? You have to have both, my daughter, to get that inner fulfilment you want. How you are going to go about having that fulfilment is entirely up to you. Personally, I will say yes, take the chance. You are not the only girl faced with such situations. When you get there, you'll see how other girls cope. You will even be better off, because I will never stop praying for you. You should not forget your Saviour either.'

So, Nko had regarded herself lucky. She had a ready-made boyfriend, she had a mother who prayed for her constantly. Her father prayed for her too, but because he was always ill, somehow Nko thought he needed her own prayers more than she did his. With all these advantages in her favour, Nko looked hopefully to the future. She knew she would have to pay the school fees of her two younger brothers, but that was something Ete Kamba would understand. An educated girl these days was not expected just to be a financial asset to her husband, but had to be so to her family as well. She would be in a good position after university, so that should not worry Ete Kamba and herself.

The smile that unconsciously spread across her face, was the smile of a girl who knew that her future was going to be rosy and sweet.

11. The Female Student

Nko tried to pull herself together as she made her way to the room she shared with four other girls; she smiled wryly to herself when she recalled what her mother had told her some time ago - that she should see how her female colleagues coped with the new situation of having to carry the old yoke of motherhood and wifehood with the new academic one. She had not really gone out of her way to ask Esther or Julia or Mrs Nwaizu how they coped with their love fives. They all infrequently made light-hearted jokes about this student or that lecturer, but when it came to the very serious topic of going steady, girls simply shied away from discussing such subjects. 'Yes, just like menstruation, a thing all of us have to endure each month, some with more pain and discomfort than the others. Yet it is considered bad manners or downright dirty to talk about it,' Nko thought. Still she consoled herself that she simply would have to be on the alert and watch for the opportunity when a girl might feel so low as to put all her defences down and talk about such things. None of Nko's friends had been that low yet.

Nko almost jumped when a bout of laughter greeted her on entering the room. It was a short lived laughter, because the girls in her room did not know that she would be so startled. She was so deep in her own thoughts.

'What, what are you laughing at?' She gasped.

The other girls greeted her question with gigglish innuendo.

113

'Still, deep waters eh?' Esther insinuated. Her remarkably white teeth lit up her dark, perfectly moulded face.

'Is it true that in your Ibibio tribe you still have arranged marriages?' Missy, the nineteen year old American girl who was there at Unical to study African culture asked. Though Missy was in the same department as Nko, she did not share the same room with her. She lived with her grandparents who were both professors in the Faculty of Education. But she spent most of her free time on campus with the other girls.

'Why, why do you want to know?' Nko asked, looking at all of them rather bleakly.

'Oh come on,' Missy continued with American directness, which many a time had taken the other girls unawares. 'We saw you, yeah we did, You were kissing and cuddling with him, your arranged partner from your village...'

'He is not from my village! He is from Mankong and he is Ibibio. And if you must know, I am Efik, we are almost two miles apart. Our relationship is not arranged, for God's sake!' Nko snapped.

'Okay, okay, don't panic. That was what I heard. But tell me, do you think someone who came from a village two miles from yours is from the other side of the world? Please enlighten me.' Missy pleaded.

Missy looked and sounded so childishly ridiculous that the other girls started to laugh.

'This is Africa, Missy. And we are talking of villages not towns. In a town situation it sounds ridiculous to say that someone from a place two miles away might as well be from the other side of the planet. In most villages, good girls are supposed to marry from their own village. Nko, in fact is very modern, seeing that though she is from Ibibio ... she's taking a man friend a whole two miles from her village...'

Nko threw a pillow at Julia, who came from Bendel State. She was from one of the minority tribes, the Urhobos. 'I thought you were on my side, You should defend me against this curious American. And for Christ's sake, I am not an Ibibio.'

"Yes and tell her that there is nothing bad in arranged marriages. Look at us; we have to spend a great deal of our allowances on clothes and expensive shoes so as to look nice and get that rich boy. Nko does not have to do that. She has her head scarf on all the time, and does not bother to straighten her hair or do her nails...'

The girls started to laugh all over again. Missy laughed the loudest, letting out squeaks intermittently. To her all this was not only strange, but fun, no doubt.

'You all sound as if you are jealous of Nko.' She said pointedly, her reddish pink lips pouting in mock innocence.

'Is there nothing like coyness or diplomacy or common tact in your dictionary? Must you blurt everything out like that?' Esther asked.

'That is what they call American honesty,' Nko put in getting her own back. 'But to be honest I have not really given my appearance any serious thought. I mean I thought I was alright or is there anything wrong with me?'

'This statement provoked more laughter. They soon recovered, and Mrs Nwaizu, who the girls called Madam, because she was married and had four children before coming to read for her degree asked, 'do you think you look different from any other students here?' Her marital status, coupled with the fact that she was reading African culture and had been a teacher for some years seemed to qualify her to ask such a direct question.

'No, I don't think so. I am simply used to tying a scarf, even when my hair is well washed and combed. I don't know why, I simply feel more secure when my head is tied, and moreover, Ete Kamba said it suits me. He said it makes me look innocent, almost like a nun.'

'Oh, for Pete's sake, I want to throw up. Can't you see that men will always put us where they want us to be? I was waiting for you to say that. Pooh, you look innocent indeed, I almost like the Virgin Mary. So you want to be a nun, enh? Then remain so, well wrapped in veils and cotton wool, completely unspoilt, simply for him. Huggh . . . huh, and you fall for it, chio, chio, chio.' Esther cried.

Missy started squeaking again. 'I don't see anything wrong with it.' She cried jumping up and down, her corn coloured hair which she wore in pigtails bounced in unison. 'I don't see anything wrong with it. I think it's rather nice, refreshing, almost romantic'

'Can you do it then?' Esther asked.

'Do what?' Missy countered.

'Go about in plain clothes, flat shoes and head scarf, just because your boyfriend wants you to, can you, Missy?'

'Hmmm I'm not really sure, but you see, I'm

different. I'm American, we do things differently in the US, and I'll look like death if I don't wear lipstick, or smart clothes. It's too hot for me to wear a head scarf in this weather anyway...'

'Well, Esther, you accused Missy of being undiplomatic: now she is being very diplomatic,' Mrs Nwaizu said, laughing.

'She is not being diplomatic, she is just beating about the bush. Missy you know you can't do it. Some men feel secure with you if you were plain just for them,' Esther began.

'But if you are plain, they won't come to you in the first place, unless it's all arranged like Nko's. I think the best thing is to look really chic, and when you have got your man, look plain to make him feel you belong to him alone. So Nko, keep your head in a scarf, and wear plain coloured skirts. But make sure you don't introduce him to me, 'cause I may snatch him from you. I look smart, you see.'

'But you can't,' put in Julia. 'They are having an arranged marriage.'

Nko flung her arms in the air, and shouted in near desperation. 'How many times do I have to tell you that we met at a church gathering. We are still friends, ours is not an arranged marriage...!'

'Don't mind us, Nko. We are being beastly.' Esther said.

'But people still have arranged marriages though, don't they?' Missy persisted.

'Yes, it is still very common among the illiterate families, but definitely not for the likes of Nko.' Mrs Nwaizu pointed out.

'So we are both right.' Missy laughed.

Nko got up, tugged unconsciously at her

headscarf, then went to the mirror that stood on Esther's bedside table. It was then that she saw Esther's marked project essay and asked accusingly, 'so you have collected your essay from Dr Madam Edet? You did not even tell me!'

'Oh, my sins have caught up with me at last,' cried Esther, placing the palm of one of her hands dramatically to her chest, and rolling her eyes heavenwards. 'I don't know how to say this, but I came out onto the balcony to tell you to go for your essay, but what did I see? I saw you kissing and cuddling, and all thought of your essay completely flew out of my head, I would have brought it for you myself, but the Dr said she wanted to see you herself. She said she had some points to talk out with you.'

'Oh don't worry, Nko. The lecturer will be there still. They work late when they have so many essays to mark.' Missy comforted. 'And you know our Dr Edet, when the spirit tells her to start marking our papers, she never stops until the spirit leaves her. And I am sure the spirit is still very much with her.'

'I know, all these religious fanatics, they make me sick sometimes. Why must she make a big show of her religiosity, I wonder?' Julia asked, directing her question to no one in particular.

'Well, if you have a neck like that, and a chest as flat as any man's, you'll like to do things that are expected of women, to tell the world that you are a woman at least. She is more proud of her title as 'Mrs' than as Dr. And as for her religious title she breathes on it.' Esther observed.

'These women are our pioneers; you must not forget that. They worked hard to achieve their academic positions, and they still would like to be seen as the pillars of tradition. What a burden! 'Mrs Nwaizu said.

'Yeah, and a burden we put on ourselves.'

'You can say that again, Missy.' Esther said, sighing at the same time.

The girls then watched wordlessly, listening to taped music as Nko ran a comb through her close cropped hair, hair which fitted her like a beret. She shook her feet out of the open sandals she was wearing and put on her only fairly high heeled shoes.

Nko made surreptitious glances at her friends who pretended not to notice her efforts. Missy could hardly keep a straight face. But before Nko left the room, Missy was glad that she did not laugh. For not only did Nko look slightly taller and more elegant, she also lost that 'I don't care if I look like a boy look.' The change was that startling.

As soon as Nko left, Missy announced that she felt awful. She now wished Nko had been left unspoilt, without any face powder and a pair of two inch heels. And in the same breath, she wanted to know if Nko would have to go to a fattening room, before she got married. As none of the other girls came from that part of the country, they could only touch the subject superficially.

Mrs Nwaizu was not sure whether people still indulged in such things. But Esther claimed to have seen some girls quite recently on television coming out of fattening rooms. She said that they were lumping and lolling like overfed seals.

Missy screamed in excitement at this piece of

information.

'You mean they came out of fattening rooms like girls in Victorian Europe used to come out for the "season"?'

'This simply shows that all human cultures are basically the same. Our mothers feed and take care of us, and at the right season, they advertise us, either in high ceilinged ballrooms or get us to dance and show off our fat bodies in the open fields, 'observed Mrs Nwaizu.

'Hmmm, it is strange really. The only thing is that in America and England, you have to starve yourself. Some unfortunate girls in their desperate efforts to be admired, end up being victims of Anorexia Nervosa. Then their parents have to pay for them to see an analyst,' Missy put in, rather seriously, very contrary to her otherwise uninhibited nature.

'If words seep out that a girl had been seeing a psychiatrist or an analyst, they would label her mad, and she would never smell marriage.' Esther said laughing.

'Ah, but it is gradually becoming fashionable to be skinny here as well, though not as skinny as the Western models.'

'And that is what I call the right kind of balance. Poor, poor woman. In my next reincarnation, I am going to be a man,' Julia said with a sigh.

'Suppose we all say, okay, I don't care. I want to look the way I am. I am fat, I remain fat, I don't care: I am skinny, I remain skinny. That I don't have to accept the dictates of society, what then?' Missy wanted to know.

'And where will you find the courage? Here in Nigeria? If you do that, they'll say you are independent, that you are a feminist, the men will run away from you.' Mrs Nwaizu said, knowingly.

'But what is bad in being a feminist? My mother is a feminist. She is married; she had me, didn't she!' Missy declared.

'We are still a long way from that yet. Here feminism means everything the society says is bad in women. Independence, outspokenness, immorality, all the ills you can think of. So even the educated ones who are classically feminist and liberated in their attitudes and behaviour, will come round and say to you, "but I am gentle and not the pushful type".'

Before Mrs Nwaizu finished her sentence, all the young women in that small room in Malabor were laughing with careless abandon. The hypocritical situation in which some modern women put themselves was glaringly obvious. And they all knew Dr Madam Edet; her ridiculous height, and her attempt to play the gentle, the innocent, the religious, the ideally approved woman. The girls here did not have to say it, they all knew who Mrs Nwaizu was referring to.

When they all recovered, Missy was determined to have the last word on what she thought was at the root of the problem. 'Why the hell can't they invent a machine or tool that can do all the loving and caring I need. Then I won't have to suppress my personality, simply for a lousy male.'

The shriek that greeted this was so loud that it could be heard from outside.

'Or better still, we do it ourselves,' continued Missy.

'Oh, Missy, if you are that desperate, a big teddy would do,' laughed Esther.

'No, that is dangerous. Just think of the headline

that will make. I'm afraid that for the time being, we are stuck with them. But my question is, must a woman be made love to, to be sane?'

'I've wondered about that sometimes.' Julia said reflectively.

But what those young women in that room in Malabor did not know was that society would like them to think that the answer was yes. And very few women bother to question it.

12. Forced Decision

Nko picked her way gingerly to Sister Dr Mrs Edet's office. She did not particularly like darkness. But this was an essay she had been waiting for. Mrs Edet was a nice person religiously, but when it came to marking essays, she always delayed them. She did her duties in bouts and stages. One fortnight it could be religious revivals, and the following week she could give glowing and inspiring lectures and do essay marking. Her students had come to know that when she was in the latter mood, it was best to exploit it, before her feelings changed again to some other thing. Nko therefore could not wait to book for a tutorial. She would go there now, and hear whatever verbal comments she was going to make, which were always better than her written ones. Few of her students could read her writing, but they were too frightened to tell her so, even though she thought she was the most approachable and easy-going, if not the best lecturer, the university had.

At her door, Nko could hear two male voices. She listened carefully and realized that one was forcefully slower than the other. She hesitated for just a second before it clicked. The slower voice was that of Mrs Edet. 'Even her voice is manly,' thought Nko and in a desperate effort to be feminine, she had to speak slowly, deliberately, producing sounds like those made by pantomime men who act as women. They were laughing now, Dr Edet and Professor Ikot. Nko could not hear the subject of their discussion clearly, but felt that it was the right time for her to knock.

'Ah, the very girl I wanted to see. Come in, Nko.' Dr Edet invited, putting in more of her artificial feminine voice which was now beginning to sound like the twang of an old guitar.

Nko somehow felt the superficiality of her jocularity, and for once was beginning to be in doubt about the standard of her work. Any other student could afford to fail or even come back to repeat, but she definitely could not. Her father was dying, and she had promised herself that she would raise her younger brothers and also look after her mother, whilst she was married to Ete Kamba. So nothing was going to come between her and her dreams. She wanted to prove that what a man could do, a woman could do also. Unknowingly Nko was setting herself a formidable goal.

Professor Ikot stopped laughing when he saw her. His eyes switched from Dr Edet on to Nko. The female lecturer noted the switch, and did not like it. She covered her feelings up none the less. Then in her twanging and now agitated voice, she went on to put Nko down, partly for the benefit of Professor Ikot. She warned Nko that she may never get a degree; that there was nothing like coordination in her essays; that her English was the worst of all her hundred and fifty students; that she should start thinking seriously about going to a teacher training college, because she did not think Nko was university material.

Her denunciations became unrestrained, and the more damaging and soul-destroying things she said to Nko, the more the latter shrunk and looked helpless, and the more the watching professor's masculine protective spirit came to the top. Watching him, and noting all his facial changes, Dr Edet got angrier and angrier, so much so that it was beginning to look as if she could not stop. Apparently her voice was going dry, for she paused to take a breath.

'I will supervise her work. I will be her coordinator,' the Elder said, in a voice that came slashing through the air, like a sharp knife.

The madam looked at him. Nko could not make out clearly what that look meant, but could see that it was totally loveless. It was full of hatred, it was a glare Dr Edet would not like to be reminded of later on when she had collected herself. Nko in her own way was sorry for herself and for this spiritual lady. But luckily she found herself tongue-tied, as if struck dumb. This was a good thing because she could not trust herself to say the right thing. How would she know what to say in a situation like this?

'I said I would supervise your work, Nko. You obviously do need help,' the professor repeated, looking serious.

'That will be ethically wrong. What about those students, brilliant ones who had been waiting for you to be their supervisor for these three years? A man of your standing should be supervising postgraduate students and you know that many students in this department would give their right hand for you to have a look at their work. Suppose those students should go and complain to their union, would they not say that you were showing favouritism?'

'I am going to supervise Nko's work,' the professor went on like a priest chanting a Litany.

With her hands shaking in unison with her voice, Dr Edet handed Nko her essay. The sheets were covered with red ink scrawls. It was then she added what seemed to Nko more of a puzzle. 'Why do you have to come here in those shoes and with a face made up like that? You have on tiro eyeliner, and you are wearing face powder. Your head is uncovered - and that cheap shiny belt . . . and you call yourself a child of God?'

'You come to my office twice a week, Tuesdays and Thursdays at eight, I shall be there waiting for you.' Professor Ikot said just as if Dr Edet had not spoken.

Hot tears almost blinded Nko as she tumbled out of Dr Edet's office. It was pitch black now, because the electricity in Malabor had failed once more.

What was she to do now? She told herself that she was still a simple young woman whose ambition was to be a modern wife with a career, and children of her own. She needed her education in order to hold the right man, and to be able to help her family. She was not so stupid as to be unaware of the Elder's interest in her. But the Elder was married to a nice quiet retiring woman, a woman who people seldom saw because she was busy having babies almost yearly. Nko knew that Ete Kamba was already becoming suspicious of the Elder's intentions, after her university forms episode. Now Dr Edet unwittingly was driving her into his arms. Would Ete Kamba be able to understand that this was simply going to be a purely tutorial arrangement? Now she was beginning to see what her mother had meant. Women like her were being presented with a kind of double yoke. She was now expected to carry the two yokes and to come out smiling at the end. 'Oh, Ete Kamba if only you could see the funny side of all this with me, then we would be able to laugh about the idiosyncrasies of the likes of Professor Ikot and Dr Edet.' Again she asked herself whether she had been right in coming to the university. And this time the answer was an unequivocal 'yes', she had been right, especially as she had now learnt that by taking a little trouble over her looks, the likes of the professor would start offering her their services. If her degree was going to cost her that much, she was going to take the gamble. Definitely she could not go back to her family and say, 'I've failed because I wanted to be a good wife to Ete Kamba.' Her family wanted success; they were not interested in how she achieved that success. 'And who am I to fail them?' Nko asked herself in the pitch darkness of that night.

13. *Apathy*

The rain was pouring this day, just like it did on most of the days in Calabar. And when it rained like this, everybody rushed in. One only went outside if one simply had to. This rain was not only heavy, it was thunderous.

In his rush to the lodgings, Isa, who clutched his few books to his chest, and covered his head with his other hand, had his head bowed. In order to reduce the distance, he had to jump over an open gutter through to the Cultural Department and then to the room he was still sharing with Ete Kamba. Isa knew all the landmarks, and knew that once he had jumped the gutter, he would not come into collision with any tree. So when he bumped into Akpan, the unexpected impact almost knocked both of them to the muddy ground.

'Why the hell can't you look where you are going?' Akpan cried.

'Me, look where I'm going, in his downpour! I can't see anything, but what are you doing in this rain? Have you gone crazy or something?' Isa asked peering closely into Akpan's moon shaped face. It looked to him as if Akpan was crying. But how could he tell when his hair was so matted, and the oil which he rubbed into his hair, together with his sweat and the rain were all pouring from his head and over his face from all sides? But somehow he knew that Akpan, that happy go lucky friend of his and Ete's, was hurt about something. He could tell from the tone of his voice; he could tell from the roughness of his language; he could tell from his red eyes and unsmiling face.

Unwittingly, Isa seemed to have caught the mood like a plague, but he had not been overcome the way Akpan was. So he could still advise gently, 'Akpan, you must get out of the rain. I know it is very warm, but the persistent tapping of these little innocent looking drops really do cause headaches, and you know people still die of something they call pneumonia in this part of the world, you must come inside and dry yourself.'

Luckily for the two of them, Ete Kamba was still at his lectures. So they had the room to themselves. Akpan mechanically accepted the towel lent him by Isa.

'Well you'll have to go to your room to change into some dry clothes. These ones are dripping wet. What is eating you anyway? If I had stood there in the rain, you would have accused me of being dramatic. Crumbs, you should have seen the figure you cut, standing out there in the rain...'

Akpan walked about the room deliberately, and then collected himself, just like an angry cat about to pounce on an unsuspecting mouse, then he made for the wall by Ete Kamba's bed and ripped down a snapshot in which were Nko and Ete. He was about to tear it into pieces, when Isa threw his whole weight on him and made him lose his balance. 'Whore! Whore!' Akpan spat. 'She is not fit to be married to a dog, to say nothing of marrying our Ete Kamba! Wait until I lay my hands on her...'

'Akpan for God's sake, what are you talking about. Ete Kamba won't thank you for this. What the hell is going on?' Isa cried, mystified.

'Eh look at you. You are supposed to call Allah, or are you not a Moslem any longer? Everybody is in a muddle these days.' With that unconnected statement, Akpan blindly shot out of the room.

Isa bent down, picked up the rumpled photograph and muttered wonderingly to himself. 'I wonder what is happening to Akpan?' I know that he was given to extreme emotions, but since I have known him, he has never been so upset... and at Nko for that matter. I wonder what that girl has done to him.'

'What are you saying, soliloquy of Hamlet or something? Must everything around you have a touch of the theatrical?'

Isa spun round and came face to face with Ete, who was still by the door wiping his muddy feet. 'I don't mind the rain, but when it goes on like this, that I do mind.' He took his eyes off his shoes and looked at Isa. Isa knew that Ete Kamba was not quite sure what he was seeing, because he walked closer to his friend and roommate menacingly, enquiringly. 'What have you done to this photograph!'

'Akpan did it, that was what I was talking to myself about. Akpan did it. I think he is mad. I saw him standing there in the rain.' Isa cried, not making much sense even to himself.

Ete Kamba was very angry, but he was one of those people who were fortunate enough to be able to master most of their emotions. There were no angry words escaping from his mouth, there was no unexplained wrinkle on his face. But his shaking hand and the studied slowness of his movements told Isa that he was upset. Isa suspected that something deeper than the two young men were willing to talk about was going on. He could understand that. After all, he was not from "these parts" as they kept telling him. He felt like stretching out his hands to reach his roommate of over two years, but he knew that those hands would be regarded as the hands of intrusion rather than those of a friend. He looked away, and watched with the corner of his eyes as Ete Kamba straightened the photo, and attempted to stick it back to the wall. The rumpled photo kept flopping and after several attempts, Ete Kamba hissed like a snake, like an unhappy woman, like a person without hope. He slowly and mechanically tore the photo into shreds and carefully put the pieces into their basket bin that was placed by the door.

Wordlessly, Isa dried himself, went out of the room and stood on the balcony. He could still see students dashing from one lecture room to the other. He could see some already making for the dining-hall. And he began to remember that day when Nko had arrived on campus, when Ete Kamba was so excited and had taken them all to Oron to see the Cross River State Museum. It was the day that that photo had been taken. The photo in which Nko had fallen into Ete Kamba's helpful arms, when the small speedboat in which they were, tipped into the water. How they had laughed, and how happy they had been. He went with Awero, and only moon face Akpan had no girlfriend. Therefore they had to fix him up with a girl, who called herself Victoria.

They had missed the one o'clock ferry. 'Look, e just de leef.' One of the boat boys had told them, pointing at the white painted ferry that was steaming along the Oron River.

'When does the next one go?' Ete Kamba asked with disappointment.

'Ah, datt one go be say 'bout five o'clock for de evening, me no fit say. But a get nice, nice, fast boat. We go reach Oron no time. The ferry go take abi say one, two hours before 'im reach Oron. But me and dis boat, thirty minutes. A cheap too. One, one naira, dat's all.'

Ete Kamba looked at the others. He and Akpan and Nko came from 'these parts', and could swim as well as any fish. For they all belonged to the Cross River State - a place in which the Niger delta divided into tiny tributaries. But Isa, Awero and Victoria, the girl '*fixed*' for Akpan all came from other parts. They were strangers.

It did not take Isa long to come to the decision that they should make the journey by speed boat. 'After all, Oron was not that far, only a few minutes.' He thought to himself. He studied the boat boys calmly and decided that if those boys could make this trip several times a day, so could he. He was there underrating the men from this area. They were small in stature, but when in water, they glided eel-like. They were masters of the rivers in their area.

It was a different story when the speed boat started. After only a few seconds on the water, its vulnerability became evident, for all to see, except maybe for the boat man. The boat was so small, and was originally designed for four or so people. But there were eight of them sitting crouched together in it. Water was splashing on them from all sides, and the noise of the engine was deafening. Everybody was in no doubt thinking of what would happen to them if a large wave should descend. A boat like that could not withstand even the tiniest one.

The panorama that opened itself to them as they left the Creeks and sped into the open river was breathtakingly beautiful. But they were all too frightened to enjoy it. Nko seemed to have been struck dumb, and Ete Kamba was looking at her and grinning sheepishly in a vain attempt to convey his fearlessness to all his friends. As for Awero, she did not bother to hide her fear. She held Isa firmly by his upper arm and shut her eyes and her ears as well, it seemed, to everything around her. Victoria, the *'fixed'* girl placed her head in between her knees and held her legs tightly. Water splashed on all of them as the boat raced along. The boat man had said it would take them only thirty minutes. But they soon realized that that was only trade talk. It took them a long forty-five minutes. The sighs of relief that escaped from everybody's mouth as the seemingly tiny houses by the Oron waterside came into view were audible and could be heard over and above that of the churning engine.

'I have never been so frightened in my whole life,' Victoria announced as her feet touched solid ground again.

'It is illegal to pack so many people in that small boat,' Akpan complained in a rare contemplative voice.

'We will have to take the ferry on our way back. It will leave about five will it not?' Nko asked.

'No, it will leave earlier, and should be in Calabar by about five. So we have a little over two hours with which to see the Museum,' Ete said, knowingly.

The Museum building was a one storey affair. Nko for her part did not really know what to expect. But one thing they all did know was that they had never seen so much local culture put together in one place. There were wood carvings, equipment for the local masquerades. The history and masquerade of the "Leopard" secret society - a group of people who elected to work like the social police in times gone by, had pride of place. There was a lot of colourful raffia and cane work of so many colours. It did not take them long to look over the whole collection. There were notices saying that the collections were much larger, but were either stolen or destroyed during the Civil war in Nigeria.

'What will people do with sacrificial masks and things stolen from places like this. They can't be of any use to anyone. They do belong here. After all the war is over now.' Awero, Isa's girl friend said musingly.

'I think those Ibos simply destroyed them out of spite. They felt we in these parts have let them down.' Ete Kamba replied.

'It is really stupid to feel like that, after all they were not winning or anything like that. And if we did not surrender to the Federal Forces, we would all have been killed.' Nko put in.

'Yes, I am glad all that is History,' announced Victoria brightly. She could not understand why university students had to be so morbid. After all, they had made the journey by boat to Oron and they had survived it. So what was there to be morbid about. She looked quickly around waiting for someone to make a comment on what she had said, but none did. She shrugged her shoulders. She really felt out of place.

She must have been mad when she accepted this blind invitation. This was not her own way of spent afternoon.

Nko and Ete Kamba were always behind. It was clear that they had much to say to one another. Isa was loyal to Awero, but they were always arguing loudly or laughing outrageously, a sort of counterfeited humour. Akpan could not be bothered about anything. Victoria could not have existed for all he cared.

They had a fight and reasonable refreshment of fried fish head and drank some sickly sweet Dr Pepper. The canteen, a big beautiful building just off the water side was cool inside. There were black studio couches covered in mock leather, lined up in military precision all around the walls. The place was clean, cool, with smiling waitresses, but rather noisy. There were these men, who were busy wrestling or playing with two faded and rather starved looking white women. Their faces were red, and their arms had red blotches all over them. They looked out of place in their equally faded dresses. In a place where women were regarded as beautiful if they were bosomy and curvy, these rather flat chested and giggly ones looked pathetic, even to Victoria who knew they were in the same business as she was. She would never debase herself like this in broad daylight and in such an open place. These women must have been so desperate, allowing these unrefined dock workers or business men to be throwing them about this way. All just because of a few naira. The men knew they were being watched, so their behaviour became more and more exaggerated. Victoria could not take any more. She stood up and announced, 'We have to go, it's nearly three o'clock.'

'Can't stand competition, eh?' Akpan asked, his Little mouth breaking into superficial laughter.

Victoria gave him a cold stare, then walked past him, and made for the main road.

At the waterside, they learnt that the ferry had broken down. It had engine trouble. Awero broke down and started to cry. 'I don't want to go back in any of those death traps again. I don't mind staying here until the ferry is repaired.'

'But that may take days.'

Again with their hearts in their mouths, another speed boat took them on. This was even worse than the first one. Because not only did it start to leak, it stopped in the middle of the river, to pick up a stranded fisherman. After that the boat man had to stand up to balance the speed boat on the river. Again it was overloaded with passengers. This one was not just splashing water on all sides, its nose was completely buried inside the gushing water.

As fate had decided that none of them was destined to go that afternoon, they arrived in Calabar safely. They all gave a yell of joy as they reached the bank, but in their eagerness to get off the boat, most of them forgot that Ete Kamba was playing the gallant gentlemen and was not going to leave the boat until Nko was safely on dry land. But her feet slipped, and she fell on to Ete Kamba's arms, thereby landing both of them in water. That was when Awero took the snapshot, remarking, 'you have been wanting to go into those arms all afternoon now I have caught you there everlastingly with my camera.'

Weeks later, when the picture was developed, it came out nice and clear, just as if it had all been planned. Ete Kamba had loved it, and had a copy pinned on to the wall near his bed with *sellotape*, hoping to have it framed one day when he was earning some money. Now he had torn the photo of that innocently risky and enjoyable afternoon into pieces.

Isa sighed and went back inside, 'it's time to go for supper, Ete. The rain has stopped now.'

His friend looked up at him blankly and replied tonelessly. 'So it has. I guess I must eat something.'

14. The Elder in a New Light

One infrequently hears people say, 'but why did you not tell us at the time, we would have been able to do something to help.' When people say things like this, they tend to forget the operative word - pride.

At the start of Ete Kamba and Nko's story, he was the king of the castle. Nko was there to tow along. This was a fact he did not have to say to his friends Isa, Akpan and the others. It was something they always knew. And when Nko was admitted into Unical, Ete Kamba became one of the elite. He was doing well in his studies, he was moderately popular, and he was going to marry a girl from his area of the country, and not just an ordinary girl, but a graduate and from the same university. His cup of happiness was apparently full.

Ete Kamba was not the one to ruin the dreams and illusions of his friends. He had been shocked by what the Elder told him, and as if that was not enough, he was almost struck dumb when he heard from Nko herself that Elder Ikot had taken the trouble to bring her her application forms when the whole campus was on strike. But what could he do? Nko's manner in telling it to him, did not indicate that she was sorry or anything like that. Perhaps it was all in innocence.

He acted as if nothing had happened. After the argument over her virginity, he learnt that he would never gain anything by arguing. But he would have it all out with her one day. He was nonetheless happy that she would be on the same campus with him for at least two years.

As for the Elder, he avoided him. He never went to his revivalist Sunday Group anymore, even though Nko kept begging him to come and keep her company. He did not understand why she needed his company.

'But you don't have to go!' Ete Kamba had snapped at her one day.

'My mother would kill me if she heard that I did not attend church every Sunday.'

'That place is not a church, it is an orgy camp.'

'Ete, please stop blaspheming. They speak in tongues and see visions.'

'They talk gibberish. The type we all talk when we make love. It is the same type of language. Psychologists have proved it you know. When one is so excited and carried away, either in the ecstasy of love making or just by simply working one's self up to such a pitch, one starts to talk funny.'

They both started to laugh. 'Oh Ete, I don't know what has come over you. You have become so cynical. You mean the early apostles were talking in that type of tongues too?'

Ete nodded. 'They were ignorant men. Mostly fishermen. And then they heard and saw and were made to understand that their Master who died a shameful death on the Cross, would live forever. They all became excited. They started talking in languages which their fellow Jews could not understand. They spoke in tongues.'

'The Holy Ghost came upon them.'

'I'll tell you what the Holy Ghost is. It is not anybody's godfather. We all have it. It can stay anywhere. Remember that "when two or three are gathered in my name I shall be with you".'

'The Devil quotes the Bible too, you know.' Nko challenged.

'So, I am the Devil now and you and your Professor, Elder, Chief and whatever title he has decided to call himself are the new saints.'

'You make our Elder the Professor sound like Idi Amin, the man with so many titles.'

'That is what I mean,' Ete agreed, 'There are so many Idi Amins walking about in Africa. All one needs to bring that authoritarianism out in them is simply to put them in a position of power. See how that uncouth Ikot had made himself your protector, because you allowed him to be. And if you are not careful, Nko, he is going to use that power over you, so much so that he will be plunging a knife into you, and at the same time be telling you it is for your own good.'

'Oh, Ete, you are getting carried away. All I was begging you to do was to come along with me, instead of playing football on a Sunday.'

Ete was worried even then. But to show it to Nko would not only look childish, but stupid as well. He had to pretend that he did not mind her going to the revivalist meetings.

He sought her out the following day, and brought the subject up again by saying.

'Nko, I'll go to the church with you if you promise to go to the orthodox one in town. The service is conducted in four languages; English, Efik, Ibo and Yoruba.'

'But those people worship as they worshipped in the dark ages. Their prayer books are full of words like "thou", and "thine" and phrases like "from thence". It has no vibrations. They don't speak in tongues and they don't see visions. It is all so clinical. I don't feel at home in such places. And those big men with their colourful families and big cars go there. We are only students; we can't afford such places yet. And the fare there and back is sixty kobo. Think of that, Ete, to spend a whole sixty kobo a day, just for transport. And when there you have to pay various contributions to many causes. It is too late to change from this one anyway. What will the Elder say?'

'Listen, this university belongs to the Federal Government of Nigeria. It has nothing to do with the Ikot family. I don't really see why the university authorities should allow this kind of thing to go on, on campus.'

'What kind of thing?' Nko asked sharply.

'Pressurizing students to come to their meetings.'

'It is only a University Christian Movement. And no one is forced to join.'

'You are!'

'I don't think we need pursue this argument. You don't want to come; God only knows why. I have to go to a place of Christian worship at least once every Sunday. I come from a Christian home.' Nko left him standing by the dining-hall door.

There was so much Ete Kamba wanted to say, and he knew he was a talker when it really came down to it. But he was suffering from fractured pride. He walked quickly up to her and asked impertinently, 'Has he been praying for you and has he seen me in one of his visions, and has he warned you against me?'

Nko's eyes opened wide and she almost smiled.

'So that was it. Simply male jealousy.' And aloud she said, 'Ete, you really overrate yourself. You think I have nothing better to do but to go to a person like the Elder and start talking to him about my boyfriend. I am sure we are going to get married, when we finish here, and I am sure you still love me, so why would I go and ask the Elder for visions about us. He does not even know that you exist.'

Here she smiled and her eyes smiled with her too. Her face told him all. He was only suspecting Nko. Not that she would go out of her way to deceive him, it was just that he was uneasy because she was too sure of herself. He had to smile back at her, and somehow he found himself kissing her good night, a thing that was seldom seen in daylight on Calabar campus. A great deal of it goes on in the dark, and under the bushes, for here the young had been taught that things like open demonstration meant corruption.

Ete Kamba would have been satisfied, but he was not. How would he go back and tell Nko the conversation he had had with the Elder? How would he tell her that the Elder had really threatened him? Nko would have laughed and told him he was imagining it all. She did not even see the possibility of Elder Ikot talking about him. But why should he blame her? Did he not think exactly like that sometime ago. Was that not the same reason he had gone to him for guidance, before he found out that he was one of those people who never practised what they preached. He had known the Elder better after that. Would it not be right for him to let Nko find out by herself? She had now got the impression that he was jealous, and all the warnings he had given were veiled and cynical. Jesus, how he wished his girlfriend had been just a simple village girl to whom he could simply say, 'you must not go to the revivalist meetings again, because I don't trust the head of the movement'. He could never say a thing like that to Nko. She would like to know all the reasons behind his orders.

Nko would have to find out for herself. Is not that what the so-called Feminist Movement was supposed to be? They said they wanted Independence, to the extent that they claimed not to want male protection. Then another thought occurred to him. 'Suppose I wasn't here, couldn't she cope with her own life?'

So he decided to leave Nko and her religion. She was free to worship her God the way she liked and he was free to pray to God privately, without any middleman like the Elder. And that, he felt justified him to play at football with his friends on Sundays.

He laboured for days with these problems, problems which he thought at first were so large and so insurmountable that no one, no one at all would understand. And when he eventually came to his decision to let Nko learn the hard way, he was glad he did, because he suddenly realized that his college work was suffering under the yoke. And that was something he would never allow to happen again. For what, in the name of God, would happen to his brothers and sisters, to his mother, to his father, to his village if after all he did not make a success of it, just because of a woman, a woman - after all you can get any of them with a few naira.

With that, Ete Kamba faced his work with renewed vigour, and the eel of doubt that was hitherto wriggling in the pit of his stomach, was choked with work.

15. Akpan's Ideal Wife

Ete Kamba had felt that he was right in not worrying unduly about Nko again. He was responsible for his parents' happiness. If he left his university without a good degree, he would never forgive himself. Nko, he felt, would always be there. He felt comfortable and secure with her. She was not one of those overdressed females tottering about in stiletto shoes with over-straightened hair and over-painted lips. Nko would always wear her simple dress, head scarf and near flat shoes, concentrating on her college work, just like himself. Both of them could not afford to fail their parents. And one other thing he was beginning to suspect was that Nko wanted and maybe loved him in a funny Westernized way. That was alright with her, but with him, he would have to remind her that even though their education was a Westernized one, he was still a Nigerian male, and had no wish to change himself. He would talk to her later about this, but meanwhile they had their examinations to get through, and during that time he was going to play the confident, non-caring role. Let Nko do the worrying for a change.

But this Sunday, the story was different. It had been widely announced that the students from the College of Technology would be playing against the Unical students. The Unical students always had their practice in the early evenings on Sundays. Nko would faithfully come and sit on the dark brown bench, just by the casuarina tree. She frequently came in her Sunday dresses, because she never had

147

time to change after the long religious affairs that were wont to be held by the Elder and Sister. And since she would have to go again in the evening there was no time for her to change to informal everyday college clothes. In any case, Nko felt that being Sunday, she had to look special, a nice change from ordinary lecture days, Ete did not have to seek her out, she was always there, and more so on an important day like this when Unical was playing against the College of Technology.

As he trotted proudly onto the pitch, laughing with his friends and fellow players his eyes went straight to the bench by the casuarina tree. There were many spectators this Sunday because of the importance of the match, but though somebody else was sitting there - a woman, it seemed from the distance, wearing a red blouse, Ete could tell that she was not Nko. Thousands of thoughts went through his mind. Has that woman sitting there pushed Nko away from her usual seat? Was Nko ill? That could not be, because he saw her talking at breakfast with her room mate and friend, Esther Cheke. He pushed her from his mind as he played hard for his team. The Unical won by a lone goal, but they were proud because the young men from the College of Technology were known to be tough players.

He avoided his friends, Isa and Akpan who he knew were looking for him to give him the usual pat on the back and tell him how good he was. They were his loyal friends and would have flattered him about this and that kick he gave an opponent. Somehow, he was not in the mood for that. He made his way straight to Hall Two, and to Nko's door.

The only occupant in the room was Mrs Nwaizu, who it seemed had taken the opportunity of this unusual quiet in their room to do some of her work. Ete Kamba was apologetic for disturbing her. And for the first-time he thought of the way he looked; dirty and wet from the rough and tumble of the match. Mrs Nwaizu did not mind, even though Ete Kamba knew she was being very nice. But when she said, "I think Nko has gone to see the Kwa Falls, yes, I am sure I heard her saying she was going to Kwa Falls."

'But Kwa Falls, is almost forty miles from here . . .' Ete Protested.

'Yes, I know. She went with your townsman, Professor Ikot.'

Even in his shock, Ete Kamba could not fail to see the mischief in Mrs Nwaizu's eyes. 'Why do they enjoy torturing us, these stupid females?' Mrs Nwaizu should not belong to that set; after all she was married to an illustrious army man. She was older than most of the students in that department, so why should she laugh at him. Ete controlled himself, and lied. 'Oh, yes I forgot. She mentioned it, and thank you, Madam for reminding me.'

Mrs Nwaizu laughed and said, 'You are very welcome. They will be back soon because of the children.'

'Which children?' Ete spun round, too quickly to hide his agitation.

Mrs Nwaizu was laughing now. 'The whole of Ikot's family went to the Falls. You know his wife has four children and is expecting another one.'

'Thank you very much, thank you.'

'She probably forgot to mention that to you, when she told you she was going to the Falls. That is rather strange, because Nko is always a direct and straightforward girl, with no nonsense about her...'

Ete Kamba felt humiliated. The humiliation was more obvious when he entered his room to see his friends and a few acquaintances celebrating the Unical's lone goal. And what was more, some of them brought their girls - girls most of them said they were not going to take seriously after leaving campus. 'But look at me, I who prided myself in having a steady woman of my own, she's gone off to Kwa Falls with another man, well, and his family.' He gritted his teeth and plunged himself blindly into a Coca Cola and cider drinking session.

Though Ete had a fitful sleep that night, he was determined not to bring the matter up when next he met Nko. He made all these decisions without remembering to think of his friend Akpan and roommate Isa. They were not deceived by Ete's forced exuberance, they noted that Nko was not present on the Sunday of the match. And as Akpan was not the type given to long silences, he had to ask his friend Ete about it the very next morning. 'I say, Ete, wasn't it strange, Nko not being there yesterday to cheer you as you played?'

'Well, we scored without her cheering us, didn't we?'

'Yeah, but look, Ete, what is the matter now? Have you two quarrelled or something?'

'We have not quarrelled, and look, Akpan, why don't you go and get your own girlfriend and leave me alone?'

I don't want a girlfriend. When I'm old enough, I'll go home and get me a sixteen year old female for a wife. I am going to want a wife, not a girlfriend. You want a wife and a girlfriend in the same woman, Nko, which is quite a different thing altogether."

Ete had to laugh. 'You are the most illogical person I've ever met, Akpan.'

'And practical. Can you imagine me mooning about like you are doing now? I would go mad. When I want a girl, I'll get one on campus, or if she becomes difficult, I'll go into town and pay some money, get all I can for my money. See? No strings attached. When I am ready to have children in order to please my parents, I'll get them to bring me a bride, again no strings attached.'

'But your wife will have a share of your life, your property, your everything.'

"Not the one I am going to marry. She won't be stupid, but will be completely illiterate.'

'Are you sure she won't be deaf and dumb as well? Because if she had eyes to watch things like television and listen to the radio... ?'

'She will see those things, I shan't be able to stop her seeing them, but I will make it my duty to tell her that those things are done by other people, you know the Europeans and the rich. And if I became rich, which I doubt very much, she would be so keen on my helping her to raise our children that she would do anything to stay with me.'

Ete looked at his friend rather curiously. He suspected that Akpan was not joking. 'You can't do it that way, not in this age. It won't be possible, and you won't be happy.'

'One funny thing about you Ete is that you have elected yourself a judge of people's happiness. Look at you, are you happy? If that girl is giving you all these emotional headaches, why not give her up and let her be the second wife of her Professor Ikot...'

Akpan was cut short in his speech.

'What did you say?' Ete Kamba growled. 'What did you say? Do you have any proof for what you just said; you had better have proof, Akpan, or else.'

'Please, Ete, let go of my shirt collar. We are no longer in school dormitories. We are undergraduates, remember. I don't know why I said that. I guess it was because somehow, during the past weeks, I kept seeing them together. People say that *Ikot* has appointed himself as her tutor. Can you imagine that? Many students would give everything to be supervised by Ikot. Look, Ete, I am sorry: But as I said, if Nko has now become too civilized for you, give her up.'

Ete let go of his shirt. He did not know that he was shaking Akpan until the latter pointed this out to him. 'I don't know what you mean by civilization. We were always civilized people. And what is bad in a girl student being supervised by the head of her department. There is no female head of department on this campus. I know she is a junior student and that the Professor should be concentrating his attention on the postgraduate ones, but maybe she needed help and he wanted to help. Nko did not tell me, but, Akpan these last weeks I have been busy with football practices and concentrating on my work. But why the hell should I be giving you a detailed account of my life. Mind your bloody business!'

Ete walked away quickly, forgetting to go for his breakfast but made his way to his lecture room.

Akpan caught up with him and said puffing,

'Ete, you are making a mistake. You said earlier that we had our own civilization before universities were built in our country. Is communal sharing of problems not one of the things that distinguished our own type of civilization? I am your friend Ete. Your business is my business. I don't think it's right for us to allow that part of our way of living to change. I know we are now carrying a double yoke of two sets of civilization. But it's left to us to make our yoke lighter by taking what is good from the new and using those things to enrich our old one. And I think communal sharing of sad emotions should stay... Ete?'

Ete Kamba smiled and added cynically, 'I know, you want to go into the village and marry an innocent girl to breed and clean for you. And I'm sure you'll want her to be a virgin too.'

Akpan laughed. 'Why not. The son of the queen of England did the same only last month. They even had to check to see whether his future wife was not only a virgin but that she could bear children. And even the mother of Jesus we all worship had to be a virgin, and few people would like to admit that Jesus had brothers and sisters ... so you see that I am not asking for the impossible. I am only asking for the ideal ... I do not mean to pry, but if you feel there is anything I can do to help.' Akpan finished seriously.

Ete patted his back and remarked, 'you are more modern than you realize. Would it have occurred to any of our fathers to say, "I do not mean to pry": they would have considered it their duty to pry, as you called it. But what you are doing now is asking my permission for you to pry. The "permission" part of it is foreign. The prying part is us, Africans. So you are bearing your own double yoke heroically.'

'I can't follow your argument. It's too early in the morning and I am hungry. We have a few minutes, why not come with me for a few akara balls?'

'No, Akpan, I'll have an early lunch. You go for your breakfast. I am glad that part of you will never change.'

'You bet. My future wife must also be a great cook. The only qualification I want.'

The two young men laughed lightly as they made their different ways to different parts of the campus.

16. Lost Innocence

Nko in all innocence was happy with her friends when they remarked on how good she was looking. She realized for the first time that subtle changes like going bare headed instead of tying one's head with a scarf could make a big impact in the way she looked. She still wore her head scarf, though only when it was necessary - whenever she was in a hurry or when the sun was too hot or when it rained. She was now so confident that whenever she visited Professor Ikot in his office, she was bare headed.

It was raining as usual, but the rain was not very heavy. She knew there were other students in the room, but she had been told to simply knock and come in otherwise she would have to wait there all evening. When inside, she saw two postgraduate students and a lecturer arguing over some departmental policy. She was shown a chair by the door and she sat there patiently as the four men eventually agreed on a policy of action. They all ended up laughing, and it seemed that it was only then that they became aware of her presence. All four pairs of eyes were directed at her. The force and the suddenness of their stare were so strong that she took refuge in staring at her shoes.

'Oh yes, I now have to supervise Nko's work, this is Nko.' Professor Ikot's voice was no doubt apologetic.

'I thought you were only a first year, maybe I am wrong, you look different, sort of grown up somehow. You share the same room, with Esther Cheke, don't you?' one of the male students blurted out.

Before Nko could fish for the right answer, Professor Ikot said, 'her work has to be supervised by me. She has chosen a project that interests me very much, and before you ask me what the project is, Colin, I'll tell you that I am not going to let you know, otherwise half the students in the Cultural would choose the same project simply to be supervised by me. I shan't be able to cope.'

Nko looked up at this untrue statement. She knew Professor Ikot was expecting his listeners to laugh at what he had just said, but none did. Instead she was greeted with another rather long and curious look. They took their leave together, but not before the lecturer addressed as Colin had said, 'I wonder how beautiful female students always manage to come up with projects so interesting, that they require the dean of a faculty to supervise.'

Nko had never felt so cheap. There was no going back now. She had chosen her path and the path was no longer hidden. The word would get round the campus soon. She had wanted her degree, she could work hard for her degree, but now everybody seemed to be insinuating that she would get it without having to work for it, simply because the head of her department would be supervising her work. Students whose work was so supervised usually come out with a good honours degree. Was such a degree worth her losing her good name, and maybe Ete? But she did not want to lose either. Then what was left for her to do when people were now telling her that she could not have both? She must either have her degree and be a bad, loose, feminist, shameless, career woman who would have to fight men all her life; or do without her degree, and be a good loving wife and Christian woman to Ete Kamba and meanwhile reduce her family and herself to being beggars at Ete's table. Oh blast it all! She was going to have both. She was going to manoeuvre these men to give her both. They thought they could always call the tune and women like herself must dance to it. With her, they were going to be wrong.

'I like the way you straighten your hair now. It gives you a sophisticated air,' Professor Ikot's voice cut through her inattention. She smiled in return.

'When people get used to seeing you come in here, they will stop talking. Campus life is like any type of community. People talk about each other. You must not let that worry you. Before you think of any project at all, you must work on your "English"; I noticed that that was what the Sister Dr Edet found maddening. We will have to spend this first semester working on that, whilst you think up topics on which you would like to base your research.'

'Thank you sir,' Nko said timidly.

'Have you ever been to Kwa Falls, Nko?'

'Pardon me, sir, what Falls?'

'We are going to Kwa Falls after this morning service; will you like to come with us. It is one of the wonders of these parts. You have to see it. The road leading to it is bad at the moment, but I will take the strong departmental car. There will be room for all of us. I shall collect you at the end of the service. Right, and meanwhile get me all your former essays, I'd like to find out why you keep translating our language into English.'

'Sometimes sir, when I try to express the everyday

things that happen here in proper Queen's English, I find that I lose the rhythm and beauty. Sometimes what I come out with is never what I wanted to express in Efik.'

'Was English a difficult subject for you when you were at school?'

'It was never one of my best subjects. I scraped through.' Here Nko smiled at Professor Ikot, and he smiled back. If anyone had told her that by talking normally and smiling like this at this man, she was encouraging him, she would have denied it completely. But this was the part of her course that had been worrying her a great deal. How was she expected to study and be able to pass down to future generations the Nigerian Culture which she would have to express in another language? She could not talk about it with Sister Edet who was much more concerned about her spiritual welfare. But Professor Ikot was capable of getting high on spiritual ecstasy and also of purring like a cat. He was purring now.

'It comes down to the same thorny problem, doesn't it? Should we put an old wine in a new bottle or go back and look for old bottles for old wines. No doubt you'll find the right amalgam after you have spent four years here at Unical. I'll pick you up at the Chapel door on Sunday. Don't bother to go for lunch, we are bringing a lunch basket.'

When outside, Nko breathed a sigh of relief. To think she had thought the Professor would make a pass at her! She tried to recall what had put the idea into her head in the first place. She was not too surprised to know that it was Ete Kamba. Ete was always jealous of the Professor. He would not tell her why, and she had stopped asking. And now she did not know how she would go to him and say that she would not be able to watch him play the College of Technology on Sunday because she was going to Kwa Falls with the Ikots. The best thing would be for her to be quiet about it. Ete was so busy with football practices that he would not miss her anyway.

It was raining when Nko dashed to the Chapel. But it soon stopped, and before the morning service was over, a timid sunshine was filtering through the watery sky. Nko went out and waited for the Professor, now the Elder of the church, by the church door.

The man came out looking a bit oily and sweating profusely in the damp air. Despite his sweat, he was still wearing that three piece Sunday suit of his. And to think that only a few minutes before, he had worn his robe of church office on top of it all - it must have been an uncomfortable affair, Nko thought.

He directed her to the waiting, white Peugeot station wagon with 'Faculty of Culture' written on both sides of it in black. The Professor was very brisk. He was grunting as if he had lost his talking ability. Nko could understand this, for had he not been talking and praying for the past hours? The man had talked himself dry. But what she could not understand and what the Professor seemed not to want to explain was his family. Nko was too surprised to ask, but was feeling better when she saw that the car was racing towards the residential quarters. So they were going to collect the family, since they had not come to the morning service. The professor's wife was seldom seen outside her home anyway.

'I hope this woman is ready with her brood.' The Professor grunted, in a voice that was a far cry from the one he had been using for his flock less than an hour ago. He jerked the car to a halt in front of their two storey 'professorial apartment'. The steward hobbled up apologetically - this race of workers always apologizes for everything. If you complained to them that it was raining, they'd come and mutter, 'sorry, sorry,' as if they had induced the rain to fall. Nko could see now that he was elaborately apologizing for something. The Professor waved him away and walked towards the car with the air of a wounded animal. He started the engine and roared into the road before announcing, 'I'll show you the Falls myself. My wife has chosen today of all days to visit her mother.'

Nko's mouth dropped wide open and her heart thumped at this announcement. As they sped along the Murtala Highway, she told herself that she could handle the situation; the only worrying thing was, 'what will people say?' and as if reading her thoughts, the Professor who was visibly relaxing asked, 'Nko, what do you think your boyfriend Ete Kamba will say?'

'He trusts me implicitly . . . em, we trust each other sir. He will understand.'

'Good, I like to see young people who actually trust each other. That is something that is completely lost to our generation. We belonged to the rat race era, an era in which almost all our education had to be paid for, an era in which there weren't enough jobs and food to go round. You people are being brought up in the age of plenty. You are the relaxed generation. Don't you think that that is the main

160

reason why you trust each other?' 'I don't know sir, I have never thought about it.' 'In our time we took things seriously. For example, I would find it easier to trust the girl I disvirgined or even the girl who would speak the truth and say, "I am not a virgin for this and that reason". But a girl who knew she was not a virgin and still wished to make me believe that I disvirgined her . . . pooh, trust such a partner . . . not me. Such girls should not be trusted for anything.'

Nko's first impulse was to open the car and jump out of it. But they had left the Highway. They were now on a narrow uneven road with deep gullies on both sides. And again she thought of her family. And she thought of these two men - Eta Kamba and this professor. She then arrived at the conclusion that she was not going to kill herself for any of them. To think that Ete Kamba had been talking about her to the professor! So this trip had been planned. Did Ete Kamba know about it? She wondered. So this was life's duplicity which her mother had been telling her about. And this strengthened her resolve the more. Was she being a silly romantic village girl when she had tailored her desires simply around Ete? After all she was now a twenty-two year old young woman. Her fault was that she was too lazy and too sheltered to get out of her little world. She had a clear picture of what the Professor would be asking. And to put it crudely it was going to be, 'if you don't let me sleep with you at any time I feel like it, you don't get your degree.' Period! And with that too she would have to put a final end to her hopes with Ete Kamba. Aloud she said nothing, even though she was aware that Professor Ikot was casting looks of triumph at her.

When she had had enough of these open glances, she gave him back a fixed smile, a smile that was nonchalant superficially, but Nko knew for the first time why some people swear to themselves that they would destroy others. Her heart was so full of hate.

At many points along the road to Kwa Falls, it became necessary for them to get out of the car and push. The road was that bad, it was that dangerous, at one time it became like an orange ribbon running in between groves of thick forest teeming with humid heat. They passed many small villages where children waved and cheered them. She would have loved the experience if it had been with somebody else She wanted to say to herself that it would have been so nice if it had been with Ete, but now she knew that her distrust had to include Ete Kamba as well.

The Falls itself was heavenly and the dwarf palm plantations that led to it were well tended. 'With plantations like this, we can never lack cooking oil, don't you think?' the Professor wanted to know.

Nko nodded.

'We are such an oily nation; oil from the ground, oil from our trees.'

Nko pretended not to hear him. And after a while the professor seemed not to care. He was going to have her, she dared not refuse, and if the worse came to the worse, he could make her his second wife. Many Christian leaders he knew in Nigeria had several wives, so what was wrong in his marrying a second one. He knew that part of the State very well. He had brought many barren women there to pray for them by the majestic Kwa Falls. Even Nko welcomed the cool, air conditioned room with toilets that really flushed.

They ate and the Professor drank spirits. She made do with Pepsi, and like a wooden doll, she let the man have what he wanted. He thundered and pushed her around and promised heaven and earth, but Nko was very still, At the end she asked, 'have you finished now? I must have a wash.' Her voice was icy.

The drive home was quiet. But when they neared the campus, Nko said slowly and clearly, 'I want a First Class honours degree. I don't care how you do it, I want a First Class honours.'

'One has to work very hard for such grades, you know,' replied the Professor, his voice uncertain.

'You mean as hard as I have worked today at the Kwa Falls?'

'Don't be silly, you must have enjoyed it.'

The sound of Nko's laughter startled the man and surprised even herself. 'You know, you must have known sir, that people are saying that you may be the next Vice Chancellor - I understand the Indian one we have at the moment will leave at the end of this semester. You being a devout Christian, an Efik and a professor, will be the natural choice and that would be really nice.'

'Yes, everybody knows that I intend to get the post, and I will.'

'You will, sir, but make sure I get a First Class honours degree.'

Nko was now out of the car. She faced the man squarely, her little face was determined. This was the type of determination Professor Ikot had never seen on the face of any woman, to say nothing of a woman so young. For a moment his face betrayed fear; Nko saw it, and how she loved that fear. 'Don't worry, sir, I won't do or say anything foolish, just think of what Ete Kamba would do: he would not believe me as you rightly guessed, but how many people would vote for a professor with a tarnished name?'

'Nko, Nko, you are upset. I should not have taken any advantage of your position. But I did not know you still took such things seriously.'

'You mean I take sex like food? That all the girls on this campus do that simply to pass their exams? I'll tell you sir that most girls here come to read for their degrees. If they become what you think, which is "prostitutes Nigerian style", it is because people like you made them so. But with me, sir, you are not going to be let off lightly.'

'But why did you not make any protest or refuse at Kwa Falls?'

'After you gave me that small lecture on virginity; I was not born yesterday. When you said that, I knew I have lost Ete Kamba. It's too late to go back now, sir. My reward is a good degree.'

'But you can't go through life using your bottom to get what you want?'

'I did not believe in bottom power until today sir.'

With that Nko rushed towards her room. She went straight to bed, faced the wall and had a good cry. She was still crying when the other girls returned from the dining hall.

She was still in this state when Mrs Nwaizu said airily, 'Nko, Ete Kamba came here this afternoon, looking for you. His team won by a lone goal and he came here to tell you all about it. I wonder why you did not tell him that you were going to Kwa

Falls with Professor Ikot and his family.'

Nko heard her voice, but it sounded like the voice of someone telling her about some legends that had long, long, faded away.

Nko saw Ete Kamba the following morning. She had to pin him down, because the young man thought she was going to apologize, and that they were going to have their usual lovers' quarrel. But she simply said, 'it's over, Ete Kamba. I have lost my innocence. Please don't ask me to explain. It is over.'

The shock of Nko's decision sent Ete Kamba back into himself. He was going to get that girl out of his system forever, and it was something he was going to achieve all by himself. Meanwhile he moved about the campus like a ghost, reverting to his old schoolboy behaviour. And just like in those days when he thought that nobody bothered or tried to find out what it was that was eating him up, he was wrong. For did not Akpan come into the room that he shared with Isa and nearly tear up the snapshot of himself and Nko? He had given himself away by going further and tearing the photo up completely. Ete Kamba was one of those people who preferred to go through disappointments privately. But his friends, Akpan, Isa and Philip would not allow him to.

When Akpan had collected himself, he went and sought out Isa in the Theatre Arts building. 'I've come to apologize for my behaviour the other day. I had no reason for treating you like that.'

'Oh forget it, Akpan. I know it is something to do with Eta Kamba and Nko, but as none of you would say a word about it, I am going to let sleeping dogs lie. In our part, we do things differently.'

'If you are going to start sounding like a wounded animal...'

'I did not ask you to come here in the first place. I only wish I could help Ete Kamba with whatever is bothering him. I know, why can't he go and have a word with Prof Ikot?

They say he is a nice man, and you know he had

been tipped as the next Vice Chancellor of this place. He is also from the same area as Nko and Ete Kamba. If I had somebody like that on this campus, I would pay him regular visits.'

Akpan's round face broke into laughter. Isa at first smiled, not knowing why his friend was laughing. Then Akpan asked him a question that took him quite unawares. 'If your honour is challenged, no, not honour; if your dignity as a person is abused, would you, Isa, swallow your pride, your right to be a man, simply because of the paper qualification you are going to get from this place?'

'That is an unfair and loaded question,' Isa began hesitantly. 'You know us Hausas, and we are what they call gentlemen of the North. We are bound by our honour, and our word is our bond, one of the reasons why the white men loved and trusted us more than you Kaferis in the South.' Isa was suddenly serious, his chiselled, near aristocratic features contrasting vividly with Akpan's moon shaped one.

The seriousness of his tone surprised Akpan. But then he had always known that people were never what they seemed. Isa struck one as a tall handsome Northerner, with the exaggerated behaviour that was expected of any actor. But that he could be serious and patriotic as well - that aspect of him was something he had kept under control. As if he were determined to match and compete with Isa, Akpan became serious too. He said, 'do you know that man, Professor Ikot, is sleeping with Nko, and I think Ete Kamba knows, or he knows and refuses to see it because he is frightened of not gaining a good degree.'

'Wallai!' Isa exclaimed. 'I won't want a girl like

that, never! Is that why he is mooning about? She is not worth worrying about.'

'I know Isa, but in our part, we the Ibibios don't let things like that go unrevenged. Even among some Ibos, not too far from here, wars have been fought because of women, you know. I don't want that man to get away with it.'

'What do you think Ete Kamba should do?' Isa looked intently at Akpan's serious face and reworded his question. 'What do you think we should do?'

A slow smile spread over Akpan's face. He got up and patted his friend on the back. 'Now I know that there is a great future for this country of ours. We must not sit on our backsides and let the likes of Ikot get away with everything. I think we should simply corner him and beat him up. We won't kill him, but we will let Ete Kamba do the beating, so that he would be in no doubt as to the reason for our un-academic behaviour.'

Isa became excited. And so was Akpan. They planned in detail what they were going to do and how. It was then that they went to Ete Kamba.

Ete Kamba was lost for words. 'But I'd like to do it. I'd like to beat him up, and I don't care what happens to me afterwards. You know my trouble, I have been brought up thinking that my certificate will be everything for me. But I never bargained for this type of thing, this challenge to my manhood. But look, my friends, why should you risk your future for my sake? What will your people think?'

'My people will think I am hero. And I like a nice punch up sometimes, especially if it is for a good cause. And I suspect that as long as we do not kill him that man will not mention it. Men like that are usually cowards: I know the sort,' Isa boasted.

'Nko stays late in the Professor's office every Tuesday night. He sees her last so that they can have a longer "tutorial" than the normal time allowed.'

They saw Ete Kamba flinch, and his fists clenched involuntarily. Akpan had to apologize and then emphasized. 'Ete Kamba, what you do with Nko after this is your own affair. You know that I always regard Professor Ikot's lectures and sermons as intellectually barren as they are assumptive of moral monopoly. I never look up to him for anything. And as for women, I am a traditionalist, oozing Ibibio purity from every pore... a no de for disi una sweety belle stuff.' He finished in Nigerian English.

'Na so for me ooo. One woman be like anoder. Why ago go kill myself for one chick, that wan pass me.' Isa added in the same vein.

Ete Kamba thanked them very much, and though he feared for his friends, he knew that they were right. Professor Ikot would not like it to be broadcast that he was sleeping with a student, because he was the self-appointed theological head of the Unical campus, and also intended to be first Vice Chancellor from that part of the country for the States University.

The sweet thought of revenge drove away all Ete Kamba's worries about Nko. 'Maybe she was enjoying it all', he thought to himself. 'For if not, why did she not put up a fight like we are now going to do.' Maybe after this, they would expel him and in his vivid imagination, he could already hear the clatter of his life's disintegrated structure. Nonetheless he was going to go through with it. He needed this personal proof for himself, for his friends and who knows, maybe for Nko. It was better than being half alive - as he had been for the past weeks.

Akpan surprised all his friends that clear and dry Tuesday evening. They all crouched by the broken desks and tables that were scattered in the main hall leading to the Cultural Department. They watched in silence as all the visitors and students who had to see the professor left. Then there was this long and tangible silence. The evening gradually gave way to the night.

A light step was soon heard. It was Nko. Ete Kamba together with his crouching friends had been waiting for her approach, but somehow he now wished she did not show up. They all saw her, her head was held high, like a proud criminal condemned and determined to go to the gallows without begging for mercy or wallowing in self-pity. Ete Kamba's heart thudded violently as he tried to see that shy girl he had met a few years ago at his village church in Mankong, in this worldly looking and sophisticated young women. Again he wished Nko had not come to this University.

Then Isa whispered, 'should we go in now?'

Akpan shook his head in the now darkened hall. They all held their breaths, wondering what Akpan was waiting for. Presently, Nko came out and Ete Kamba's heart sank because he thought that he was going to beat up the Professor in his office with Nko watching. Akpan was allowing them to wait too long. He was sure that soon Professor Ikot would come out and they would have lost their chance. Then he stopped thinking as he saw in the dark that Nko was not carrying the new shoulder bag she had started using as a mark of her new image. And then he noticed something else, Nko was not walking towards the door, she was going towards the loo, but she left the Professor's office door half open. The whole hall was that empty, dark and quiet, that Nko and the Professor behaved with the confidence of two people who knew that they were completely alone.

When the loo door was shut, Akpan signaled his friends to come out of hiding. They rushed as if the three of them were one man, into the Professor's room. He had a short sleeve shirt on and that was all.

He opened his mouth once to shout or talk, but Ete Kamba gave him one. Blood spurted from his large nose, and Ete Kamba wanted to give him more, but Akpan told him to wait. Nko came in looking like somebody who had completely rejected herself. Her eyes opened wide and her hands went to her mouth as she saw what was happening in the room. Isa and Akpan forced her into a chair and let her watch as Ete Kamba used the professor as a punch bag. The man was too scared to defend himself, he could only protect his face. The boys smashed his glasses and when Ete Kamba saw him wilting as if he were unconscious, he tore his shirt from him. Then he heard Nko's subdued sob. It was then he became ashamed of himself. He did not know that he had bottled up so much anger. Professor Ikot was now stark naked; he was bleeding; he was peeing; he was dribbling; his breath smelt sour and Ete Kamba felt revulsion.

Then Nko started to beg the boys. 'Please, Ete Kamba, stop. He'll die and they will accuse you of murder. Please, I don't want you to kill him because of me...'

Ete Kamba turned round fiercely, slapped her on

both sides of her face an snarled at the same time. 'If I kill him, it's not because of you, you cheap whore, I am killing him because I am a man. Why don't you tell your confessor to hit me back?'

Nko snarled back at Ete Kamba. She had nothing to lose now. But one thing she was going to hang on to was her individuality and dignity. She was not going to let these men mess up her emotional life. She knew she had lost them both, that did not worry her much. But none of them was going to make her feel guilty. After all she originally came to this university to get a degree. She squared her shoulders and looked at Ete Kamba in the face. 'You call him my confessor, but what of you? Who told him how we met and all that, enh? Answer me, Mr Holier than thou. Did you tell your friends that, enh?'

Ete Kamba seemed to be shrinking. And as for the professor, he crouched and covered his face, ready for more blows from Ete Kamba. Ete Kamba was too shocked to speak for a while. His friends looked blank, they did not seem to grasp the importance of what Nko was saying, and Ete Kamba was not going to enlighten them. He soon recovered himself and collected a large foamy saliva and spat it plop on the Professor's head.

Nko spat back at Ete Kamba. 'I am not asking you to understand. But if I am a whore, you two made me one. Always remember that.'

'Let's go now,' Akpan said in a tired voice.

Isa bent down and collected the Professor's trousers, his torn shirt and even his shoes and said, 'in case you think of reporting us.'

'And I am keeping this as a souvenir,' Ete Kamba

said as he fished out Nko's cream underpants which she had stuffed into her shoulder bag. He looked challengingly at Nko, maybe expecting her to fight for it, for what he regarded as her last shred of honour. Nko did not bother. She had heard Akpan's tired voice, and she wanted them to go without any more fuss.

Ete Kamba's last move made them all grin mischievously as they left. It made a strange picture - the naked Professor had his head on his desk, his eyes roaming with fear; Nko sitting opposite him, her face averted.

The male students walked back into the dark night and went to Isa and Ete Kamba's room and waited. They did not actually know what they were waiting for. After a while Akpan asked, 'do you think he will die?'

'Of course not, people like him don't just die like that. He's too wicked to die. Even the devil won't have him in hell. But, Ete Kamba, you are a wicked soul. Why did you keep punching his balls?'

'So that he can never perform again, the stupid bastard.' Ete Kamba replied neatly.

The young men laughed wickedly.

Nko had thought that she would slide into her room unnoticed by Esther and the others. But she was wrong. Mrs Nwaizu, who because of her age and experience had assumed the role of a big sister for the girls, confronted Nko by the door.

'Where the hell have you been?' She demanded.

Nko saw Esther standing at the other end of the room in her cotton nightdress her arms akimbo nodding like a lizard to every word Mrs Nwaizu said. 'We could not lock our door, and you know perfectly well that some of us have early lectures tomorrow.'

'Please let me in first,' Nko said dejectedly. 'Let me in, please. I may have to leave this university anyway.'

'Yeah, you do that and make it quick, but don't go about giving the rest of us a bad name. You know how news, especially bad news about female students spreads in this place. Must you stay this long with Professor Ikot? What type of tutorial are you having with him anyway? Midnight tutorial?' Julia demanded sitting up in her bunk bed and flailing her arms up and down like a tired windmill. 'If this happens again, I am going to tell my parents, I swear.'

Nko buried her head in her bed and began to cry. The others did not know what to say. Then Esther who had been studying the whole scene, pointed and mouthed inarticulately to the others at the blood stains that were on Nko's yellow dress. Mrs Nwaizu's normally large eyes became larger. She went to the door to make sure it was locked and that they were not being overheard. 'What happened to your dress, Nko? All this blood . . . have you been in a fight or something?'

Nko could not answer for a while. She went on crying spasmodically, and the sight of her thus, stirred the pity in the other women. Mrs Nwaizu sat by her and lifted her head to make sure she had no bruises. She said, 'Alright, alright, Nko, tell us what happened. But if you don't want to, we won't mind. We were worried about you, with the campus being so dark, you know NEPA and all that.' As for Julia and Esther, they were burning with curiosity.

Nko knew that the others would understand her plight and that it was better for her to tell them herself. She was sure it would be all over campus in the morning. She started telling the events of the evening in between sobs, but by the time she got to the middle, she realized that she had become the heroine of a dramatic story.

'You mean Professor Ikot actually begged for mercy? I always hated that greasy man,' Julia declared.

Esther wanted to know why Nko did not call them, even though she had said that she did not know it was going to happen. Nko was expecting condemnation from her roommates, but none came. She did not mention that she had ever had sex with the Professor, but she guessed that they knew. Some of them were in the same boat, but many could refuse because they were clever enough to know that they could make their way without seeing any Professor or lecturer outside lecture hours. Nko's life had been too sheltered, and she now knew that she had been stupid. She ought to have told her friends. She knew now that there was nothing to be ashamed of. Their general attitude was that if they reduced them to using their sex to get their certificates, then that was what they were going to do.

'But that is rather unfair,' cried Julia bitterly. 'I want a good degree, and I am going to work for it. That is the joy of being here.'

'That is one of the joys of being here,' Mrs Nwaizu corrected. 'We all want to work for our papers, but what do we do, when men old enough to be our fathers come round to tell us that we can't get it unless we have their lousy "tutorials"?'

This was greeted with shrieks of laughter. They all forgot that it was past midnight.

'Anyway you can make it up with Ete Kamba now. You must explain to him why you did what you did. That your family would suffer if you went home without a certificate,' Esther began.

Nko shook her head. 'I have lost him. Do you know he told the Professor that he was not sure I was a virgin when we first made love?'

'Really, I thought he was intelligent. Eh, was he blind? Did he not see the blood?' Mrs Nwaizu asked in mock seriousness.

'We did it by a wall, and he wanted enough blood to float his whole village.' Nko sniffed laughing.

'Did you ask him if he were a virgin too?' Julia wanted to know.

They were all laughing now. Then Nko said, 'but that is not the point. The fact that he could discuss a thing like that with another man, put me right off him. I feel a thing like that is private.'

'Maybe he told the Professor as his religious confessor, and that rogue had to tell you to spite

Ete Kamba. I hate him, I hate him.' Esther cried.

'You mean Ete Kamba had to tell a confessor so that he could pray to God to make Nko a virgin again? Honestly, our men are so childish. When will they wake up. But personally, I should talk to him : I still think you should. He is so very handsome, and struck me as intelligent, for a man, you know.' Mrs Nwaizu said.

'No, don't. Must you marry him anyway? Must you marry at all if you don't particularly want to? Get a good degree, by working hard for it. It is easier to get a good degree using one's brain power than bottom power. They may try to tell you that your bottom power is easier and surer, don't believe them. What is more nauseating in this world than having to put up with that greasy man with decaying body and abundant belly. Seeing his hairy paws on my essay papers makes me want to throw up. Nko, you don't have to lower yourself to that level. You are young, you're a beautiful girl. What's the matter with you? Pooh, Professor Ikot! He makes my skin crawl,' Julia declared flatly.

'And by the way, Nko, how did he get home?' Esther asked.

Before Nko could answer they were all laughing helplessly. Nko laughed the loudest as she remembered the sight. She replied, 'I helped him down the stairs, to his car. He was in pain all over. He asked me if I had a scarf or a lappa with me. I said, "no," that I had only a belt. He ignored me, fumbled for his car keys, but they were in the trousers the boys took. So he got out, and started to walk like a drunk, like those mad naked men we see about. In fact you would have taken him for one.'

When they had all stopped laughing, Mrs Nwaizu advised. 'I don't think you should contemplate leaving the university. You are a nice girl. If you become promiscuous, which you are not, our men made you so. If he makes a case out of this, then that is different. But I am sure that he will not.'

'But how will he explain what had happened to him to his family, his driver, to everybody? I am sure he'll be ill for weeks,' Julia said.

'They'll probably think he's drunk. We'll have to wait and see. Nko, can you manage lectures tomorrow?' Esther asked.

'No, no, you should stay in. We'll come and tell you what the rumour is. If it's too bad for you to live down, you could go home for a while. Nko, do put me out of my misery. How can you make love by a wall?'

'Oh shut up, you curious bitch,' Esther said as she started to pound on Julia.

'Are you a virgin then, Julia?' Mrs Nwaizu asked laughing.

'I don't know. Our house boy tried it once with me. He went half way though. I remember it well, because I was screaming. I think I was six or so. My parents went to London, and I was left in the house with my brothers and sisters.'

'Oh, my God. Confession is good for the soul. You mean you knew a man when you were six years old.'

'I said around six.'

'Well, my dear girl, there is no half way. You are not a virgin. Your father's house boy had done it.' Mrs Nwaizu said harshly.

'But that is unfair. I have been preserving myself. I

allow petting but nothing more and I did not bleed or anything at the time.'

'Oh shut up, for God's sake, Julia. You are so green. How can you bleed, when you've probably burst the blood bag before it was ready. You are preserving nothing! Let your boyfriend - the German boy doing Tropical Medicine, is that him... well try it with him. I hope he is circumcised though. Many of those white men are not circumcised, so they hang down like wet intestines. Hughgh!'

'And their women are not clitorised...awful.' Nko said.

'Well, different people, different customs; Nko, just keep a low profile meanwhile.'

'But, madam, am I a virgin?' Julia cried pathetically.

'I am sorry to shatter your dreams, girl. Virgins don't make good wives, not always. They are too cold. So go to sleep, Julia.'

Nko kept a low profile for a couple of days.

20. Double Yoke

Two days after the confrontation in Professor Ikot's office, the Unical Herald carried a rather curious article. On the front page was Professor Ikot in a dressing-gown giving an interview to a reporter. He said that whilst he was working late in his office, he was attacked by these thieves, who beat him up and would have stolen his car but for the fact that he gave them what they deserved - his great punches. He expressed himself fluently in his biblical rhetoric and said that but for God's grace he would have been a dead person by now. He displayed his battle wounds and told the reporters to go to his office and see for themselves.

To the surprise of Ete Kamba and his friends, Professor Ikot became a hero. Police officers were deployed from the town's main barracks to search for clues; all the suspects and well known criminals in town were locked up for questioning. The governor of the State talked about the security on campus, and apologized on behalf of all the Calabar people to the Reverend Professor.

Nko and the women students who knew the truth could, not believe their ears. That a person could turn such adversity into fortune. Most of the students knew what had happened by now, but nobody would dare mention it to any of the lecturers.

A few days after, Mrs Nwaizu said to Nko, 'why keep a low profile, get on with your lectures. We were right, weren't we, he did not have the courage to own up.'

'Do you know that they are now going to give him

some bodyguards to protect him, because it is now clear that he will be the next Vice Chancellor?'

'Oh, God help us.' Mrs Nwaizu laughed. She then asked after a pause, 'have you made it up with Ete Kamba?'

Nko shook her head. 'I don't think we ever want to see each other again.'

'Pity to let such a pig ruin your life.'

'Yeah, he has ruined our lives, you see, madam, I am even going to have the beast's baby. And I am not going to abort or anything. It should arrive during the next long vacation. My people will be shocked, but they will forgive me. One thing they are not going to hear from me is the name of its father. I am going to make it clear that it is not Ete's child.'

'I am sorry, Nko. Now you have to work even harder. Because you know the more children you have, the harder you have to work.'

'I am having only this one.' Nko found herself laughing. And then asked, 'but where is that girl whose only dream was to be a good wife and a mother? Has she gone forever?'

'No, she has not gone. She has simply just grown because she is going to be a sure academician and a mother. You are still going to have a double yoke to carry. You can't escape it, you are a child of this age, Nko.'

As for Ete Kamba he watched helplessly as Nko became big. He avoided her, and she seemed to have acquired a kind of independence. If only she would go away and hide her shame. But if he had asked Nko that question she would have replied sweetly, 'but it takes two to make a woman a prostitute.'

All this happened four months ago, before this new madam came. So, as Ete put a final full stop to his essay, he felt a sense of relief.

'I have enjoyed reading all your creative works. I am glad to note that most of you used your experiences to make up your stories. You'll be surprised to know that many famous writers write autobiographically. Because of this I would like to discuss your work with you individually,' Miss Bulewao said.

Ete Kamba knew he would have to go to her office when called. It had never occurred to him that he could discipline himself to write and make such a high grade.

The lecturer invited him in her pleasant assuring voice to come in when he knocked. He sat down and without much ado she said to him, 'Why don't you ask your girl to marry you and why don't you talk to her?'

Ete Kamba at first felt like going straight at Miss Bulewao and throwing a chair at her. The woman was asking him to go back to a girl who had shamed herself, and who despite all that was parading her shame all over campus. He controlled himself and replied gutturally, 'Never!'

'Passing from childhood to adulthood is a long and painful process. And one of the golden rules one has to learn in that process is this - try to put yourself in place of the other person. How for instance did Nko know of your interview with Professor Ikot?'

'He told her himself, I think.' Ete Kamba's voice was distant.

'Did Nko know why you had to go to him?'

'No, madam, I never had the opportunity to explain.'

'So, do you think it's too much trouble to try and explain to her, why you did what you did?'

Ete Kamba was staring at her vacantly.

'And when you had sex with her by the wall, were you a virgin yourself?'

Ete Kamba felt like getting up and walking out of that office. These people who had stayed too long overseas tended to lose touch with reality. He was the man, why should he be a virgin?

'You find that too difficult to answer?' Miss Bulewao was smiling. 'The average modern Nigerian woman is almost priceless. Her family comes first. She works hard, and if she is well educated like Nko she will be a good companion as well. And to think that you more or less grew up together, and you still love her . . . where will you find a village girl that will replace her. Suppose you get a village girl and she is not a virgin, what will you do?'

Ete Kamba got up, wanting very much to tell this lady to mind her own business. But then he heard himself saying something that at first sounded as if it was coming from somebody else. 'I don't really care if Nko were a virgin or not. But this child she is carrying...'

'There, you are growing up, Ete Kamba. When did you realize you were no longer looking for a virgin to pluck? After writing your story perhaps? You know something, many of our men, I am sorry to say never reach this stage of reasoning until they die in old age. Well I am glad. But, Ete Kamba, suppose by mistake one of the girls you sleep with on campus becomes pregnant, and you don't want to marry the mother because you don't love her; how will you feel if Nko rejects you on that account?'

'Madam, you seem to be forgetting that I am a man. I can do what I like. A man can raise his own bastard, women are not allowed to do that.'

'But young man, Nko is going to be a graduate from this university. She too can afford to look after her own bastard. Or you mean to tell me that having children out of wedlock is another masculine preserve? I know your problem. You are wondering what people would think of you. You think they will say you have gone soft in the head, or as our mothers used to say, that, that woman has given you some love meat to eat and you can no longer think as a man. Our people think that only women should be loving and maybe forgiving, and that a man who does that must have eaten his wife's love meat. You must have heard of Hitler. They say he loved cats and music. Can you imagine that? Only men with large hearts can love and understand. That does not make them weak. It makes them great.'

Ete Kamba shook his head. He did not agree with Miss Bulewao.

And for once, there was a near irritation in her voice. 'Then why are you unhappy? And why are you lying to yourself? Because of your parents maybe? But they have their own lives and Nko would always respect them because you came from the same part. Ete Kamba the question is - are you strong enough to be a modern African man? Nko is already a modern African lady, but you are still lagging ... oh, so far, far behind.'

Ete Kamba as usual, avoided his friends after this long talk with Miss Bulewao. He would think seriously about writing. He would teach and write at the same time, and if his father complained that teaching was not a prestigious life, he would have to explain to him that he needed the long holidays to be at his typewriter.

But as for Nko and himself, fate lent a hand. Esther ran to him one Sunday, breathing heavily. 'It's Nko,' she panted. 'She wants to kill herself; her father has just died. We just can't reach her.'

'Good evening, boys, do sit down. Today we shall explore the possibility of working on biographical details, to make them look fictitious. Ete Kamba, Ete, you have to start...'

There was no answer. The class was silent, only the humming of the fan could be heard. Miss Bulewao lifted her head and asked, 'but where is Ete Kamba today? It is important for him to be present at this lecture.'

Akpan got up rather reluctantly, and very apologetically said. 'Please, madam, Ete's friend has lost her father, and he went to her village with her. He'll be here for the next lecture.'

Miss Bulewao looked fiercely round the class to see whether any boys would laugh or make some canny remarks. 'It's nice to know that many of you are bearing your double burdens or yokes or whatever heroically. The community burden of going home with the person we care for to bury her dead, and yet the burden of individualism - that of knowing that we are happier in somebody's company, however tainted we may think he or she is. Women do have to make these decisions too you know.'

'Give me a fourteen year old village girl with uncomplicated background any time,' Akpan said in a remote voice, just like someone in a dream.

'You are in a dream world, Akpan, do wake up.' Miss Bulewao said to him.

The class laughed as they saw him startle into wakefulness.

'Fancy doing your wishful thinking aloud and in the class,' Philip said.

This provoked more laughter.

Poor Akpans of this world!

By the same Author

In the Ditch
Second-Class Citizen
The Bride Price
The Slave Girl
The Joys of Motherhood
Destination Biafra
Naira Power
The Rape of Shavi
Kehinde
Gwendolen
The New Tribe
Head above Water

Children's Books

Titch the Cat
Nowhere to Play
The Moonlight Bride
The Wrestling Match